HEROES ARISE

LAUREL ANNE HILL

Illustrated by
JASMINE NAKAGAWA

KOMENAR
publishing

Cover design by KOMENAR Publishing and Trevor Yormick
Interior design by BookMatters

HEROES ARISE. © 2007 Laurel Anne Hill. Illustrations © 2007 Jasmine Nakagawa.

Special book excerpts or customized printings can be created to fit specific needs.

For information, address KOMENAR Publishing, 1756 Lacassie Avenue, Suite 202, Walnut Creek, California 94596-7002.

Library of Congress Cataloging-in-Publication Data available

ISBN 978-0-9772081-4-2

FIRST EDITION

10 9 8 7 6 5 4 3 2 1

Printed in the United States of America

To my husband David
our daughter Alicia
my stepsons David, Jim & John
my daughters-in-law Kathy & Lynn
my sister Kathleen
my brother Douglas
my mother Verna
my grandmother Mabel
my granddaughters Julie, Kelly & Lisa
and all the other heroes in my life

ACKNOWLEDGEMENTS

I would like to acknowledge and express my heartfelt thanks to the following:

My husband David, for his love, inner strength and total commitment to my writing dream.

Charlotte Cook and the rest of the amazing KOMENAR Team, including Jasmine Nakagawa, Alan Morris, Julia Tanner, Clarissa Louie, Lydia Scott-Adams and Elisabeth Tuck. KOMENAR trimmed and sculpted my unruly bush of words, allowing branches to strengthen and flower.

All others who reviewed my manuscript, especially John Randolph, Lee Paulson, Jill Hedgecock, Leslie Burton, Laura LeHew and Trish Henry.

The guest authors of RavenCon 2007 and BayCon 2007 who offered me encouragement and advice, particularly Robert J. Sawyer, Allen Wold and Peter W. Prellwitz.

Also *Chris Moore*, for his philosophy about ropes, first-aid and life. *Josh Josephson*, for his valuable information about mountain climbing. *Janice Fong*, for her imaginative poster to keep me focused. And *Tom and Claudia Corona*, for introducing me to Charlotte Cook years ago.

All my other friends, family and coworkers who believed in me, especially Herb & Maggie Zeller, Kevin Mills, Shawn Mills, Terry Grimmer, Teresa LeYung Ryan, Robyn Roberts and Lillian Sparks.

HEROES ARISE

If vengeance swallows the land,
Tharda shall bring a white light to give strength to the least of us,
and unbelievers will make heroes arise.

TARR

THE RAIDER

CHAPTER ONE

A BLOOD ALLIANCE

Gundack glanced back into the darkness. His caravan of drivers and sandship lizards had settled for the night and now only awaited his return at Jular Plateau. He would join them again when he had concluded his business at the merchant encampment before him. Crumbled rocks encountered on the climb down irritated the webbing between his toes. Less bothersome though than the predictions of that soothsayer. A human, not a fellow kren, held vital information, if not his very future. Not a desirable situation. Humans were so unpredictable.

Scant moonlight coated the animal-skin tents at the merchant encampment. A jagged black line marred the sloped roof of one tent, the disfigurement like a claw wound festering with rot. The mental association did not bode well. This was the merchant man's enclosure. Gundack's transcendent associations and abilities to read fellow beings had often been the difference between success and failure, life and death. But clicked signals of alarm to his tribal kin would not span the distance between Jular Plain and the caravan. He had traveled too far to let potential danger dissuade him.

Gundack grasped the edge of a weathered hide tent flap, pulled the drape back, and ducked his cowl-covered head and broad torso. He stepped from darkness through the tent's narrow portal into modest luminance and warmth. His shoulder jiggled an inner hide flap, and the crust on his head scales prickled. Something unusual—an object with power—must have brushed against his hood. He looked up. A braid of gut thread dangled from above. An amulet. If only a talisman's touch could resolve his pressing matter of the heart.

Quivering light arose from a thick, white candle on the tent's floor. The glow bathed a human's slender form, the man dressed in a dark robe. The bearded merchant sat cross-legged on a woven mat, eyes half-closed and palms cupped over his exposed knees. He neither looked up nor spoke, as though in some sort of stupor. Mixed aromas of incense and musk filled Gundack's nose. He scanned the tent. An ordinary walking stick tipped with a trenching spade was the only potential weapon. How unusual for a merchant to travel without a spear or long knife. Especially a human traveling among desert and mountain krens. And where were his sacks of goat hides or metal goods, the items he would have brought to this encampment to sell?

The candle flickered, raising Gundack's attention to the shape on the hide walls. Such an insignificant shadow this human cast. Barely half the size any kren's frame would make. A single stroke of Gundack's claw hand could rip open the human's belly as easily as a kreness' blade slashed overripe melons. But no reason to harm this merchant from the northlands. At least, not yet. Attacking a weaker opponent without good cause would bring dishonor. Besides, the human with charcoal-black braids and smooth hands browner than cragweed tea would soon discover hidden knowledge. Or so soothsayers had claimed. That secret could prove more valuable to Gundack than starstone mines in the nearby Divider Mountains.

Starstones. He had more than enough of those sparkling deep blue gems to negotiate the dowry of Eutoebi, the bride of his choice. She would use those stones to support her elderly father. Her father in turn would bless their marriage, allow them to begin a life together and raise krenlings. As many as the gods would allow. No, money wasn't the problem he faced.

"Peace be with you, brother trader," Gundack said in the language of the Northmen. His tongue rolled into an awkward curl as he spoke. Gundack should have formed Northmen words with ease. Human and clawkren faces were similar in structure, though krens had boxier jaws and broader tongues. Yet syllables seemed to pour through his nose, even after all these years of practice.

The merchant man blinked as though awakening, then stared up at Gundack, raising his hand toward his mouth. Did Gundack's stature and claws intimidate him? Kren skin, green and brown, blotchy as fermenting kettlefruit, made some humans uncomfortable. Their external covering was so monochromatic and uninteresting in comparison. More like the chalks among his own kind.

Gundack repeated his greeting. He extended his friendship arms, the smaller two of his four. He slumped his shoulders, bringing his battle appendages to rest against his sides. His ropy tail relaxed and uncoiled. Gundack's speech might sound strange to this human, but his body would not project a threatening message.

"You must be Gundack of the Red Sands," the human said in Sandthardian, the dialect of Gundack's desert tribe. Mistimed tongue clicks and ineffectual throat growls punctuated his words. His pink lips spread in a crooked smile between his mustache and whiskered chin. "I've been waiting for you."

Gundack pushed back his hood and studied the human's odd smile. The merchant man had known he would seek him out? Whispers certainly traveled with speed in the deserts and mountains of Thard. Or, had this human used mottleflower in recent days and received visions from the gods? Gundack's ears tingled and flattened against the top of his head, an instinctive reflex when something felt wrong. Did mottleflower intoxicate the human now?

The merchant man leaned forward, arms spread, and rose from his cross-legged position to standing. What remarkable balance. Even Eutoebi, a most graceful kreness, could not have accomplished this agile maneuver. He also had great strength in his upper legs, although human muscle power could not match a kren's.

Gundack's ears tingled again. He tightened his stomach muscles. His friendship arms remained extended. This human's help was essential to close a tent flap on the past and open another to his future. Gundack must not demand information before the right time. Water dripped into desert wells at its own rate. He gave the customary hand signal that they should each speak using their own native language and encouraged the man to begin.

"Let me introduce myself properly," the human said.

The merchant rested his rough, callused palms against Gundack's upturned friendship hands. How unusual. He offered to open his mind to transcendent perception, the way a kren would. Gundack grunted. He read the human through body warmth, odor, and movements of his hazel eyes. Yes, the man understood and welcomed this custom. Gundack slowed his breathing and felt the man's wrists for his life pulse. How easy it was to find a human's pulse. Krens had thicker skin, like leather in comparison. Gundack concentrated, stretching his mind, flowing with the man's blood to that deep well of thoughts behind the eyes.

This human was not on a journey to buy or sell wares. No wonder sacks of merchandise didn't crowd this tent. A flash of images. Tarr, the raider kren. Tarr, Gundack's enemy. Another kren, a young male reminiscent of Kan, Eutoebi's brother. Wretched Kan.

Such fleeting images. Were these visions distorted, or had they arisen from the depths of Gundack's own mind? And the merchant man guarded many of his thoughts. Still something more. Strength. Focus. Love. This human, too, had a mission. Perhaps one of honor, as well.

"What's your name?" Gundack said. "And what really brings you here?"

"I am Rheemar," the merchant said, his voice low and nasal.

He added no name of his home city or village. Was this human more nomadic than the wandering tribes of the desert clawkren? Gundack tightened his friendship hands around Rheemar's. The human's crooked smile returned.

"Like you," Rheemar said, "I have a vow to fulfill." The man's pulse pounded against Gundack's touch. "I seek to destroy Tarr of Larmon."

Gundack's heartbeat quickened. His perception had been correct. Tarr. The one who could vanish at will in mountain mist. Now an image from his own life—green and chestnut flesh engulfed by funerary flames, the body of Gundack's slain wife. Tarr had murdered Talla ten years ago, during a raid of her tribal encampment. Gundack had hunted him ever since, on every trading foray. But Tarr had evaded him. Three moon cycles ago, soothsayer krens had foretold a merchant man would soon discover Tarr's winter hiding cave. That was why Gundack had traveled here to Jular Plain, where merchants often gathered.

But the soothsayers had mentioned nothing about the merchant's own desire for vengeance. Something they had not noticed in their visions? Or, something that simply wasn't there. Tension coiled his tail. Rheemar could be part of a trap set by Tarr or another mountain kren with a grievance against desert tribes. Gundack studied the amber lines in Rheemar's pupils and felt the texture of his palms.

"What is your quarrel with Tarr?" Gundack asked.

The human's pulse throbbed with a steady rhythm, neither too fast nor slow. And his odor contained no hint of fear. Yet calmness could be feigned.

"Three years ago," Rheemar said, "two moons before the season of sandstorms, Tarr raided my village." He glanced down, toward the woven mats on the tent's hide floor, then up at Gundack. Fury appeared in the human's deep-set eyes, like flames leaping from a runaway fire. "Tarr carried off my younger sister. I know not where she is now. Where he is, either."

Gundack grunted. A young sister taken. But Rheemar hadn't yet discovered Tarr's hiding cave. Too bad. Not the news he sought. Gundack's own hunt for Tarr was widely known. After all, even breezes had carried the tale of Talla's savage murder to all provinces of Thard. No wonder the merchant had waited for Gundack.

The backs of Gundack's ears tingled again, even more than they had before. Something about this human and his story didn't match. Gundack's friendship hands released their grip on Rheemar. He had perceived all he could by touch tonight. Time to read the human's words.

"I suspect," Gundack said, "you've heard what Tarr did to my Talla. How I vowed to avenge her and must do so before I remarry." Should he confide more? No, details would only heighten Rheemar's concern for his sister. "I understand your loss and fears. We must discuss our needs kren to kren, according to customs of the Red Sands."

"Do you mean for me to speak in your own language, after all?" Wrinkles pleated the human's forehead. He tilted his oval head to one side, his expression like that of a krenling puzzled by addition and subtraction.

"Continue speaking in your tongue of comfort," Gundack said. "But let your lips form words of truth."

"Oh," Rheemar said. "Now I understand. We need to share tea."

Gundack glanced around the tent. A metal water pot sat on heating stones in one corner. No steam seeped from under the lid. The human gestured toward the vessel. Rheemar knew another important clawkren custom. In the Red Desert, all serious discussions began with sharing tea.

"You take care of the water." Gundack patted the tea pouch tied to his money belt under his robe. "I'll ready a leaf."

Rheemar grasped the water pot. Both pot and stones would need warming in the campfire outside. The human's black braids swung as he ducked his head through the tent's portal and exited. Gundack removed his hooded cloak and laid the linen on the tent floor. He extracted his tea pouch from under his robe and arranged the medley of pungent, dried leaves on the light brown cowl.

Cragweed would not do today. Cragweed was prized by desert clawkren but often sickened humans. And black nodule sprout might be too bitter. He fingered a curled, yellow leaf with sharp, jagged edges and a faint sweet aroma. Sugarthorn from the northland, larger and more robust than the mountain variety. He would offer this one when the merchant came back with hot water.

Gundack slipped the other leaves into his pouch, holding the cragweed longer than the rest. Cragweed tea was served to seal marriage contracts. Eutoebi would prepare it for him if he succeeded and survived this ordained pilgrimage. And if she continued to honor her vow. But would he return to his home tribe in time for the day of marriages this year?

ﺵ ﺵ ﺵ

Gundack knelt on a straw mat, his legs parted. He leaned back against his heels. His tail uncoiled and stretched straight. A ceramic bowl of sugarthorn tea warmed his friendship hands. His claw hands rested beside his knees. This was the customary stance when those with honor discussed issues of leadership, strategy, alliances and customs.

Rheemar knelt and faced Gundack. He shifted his weight from one knee to the other and back again. Tea sloshed in his bowl, like incoming tides against a shoreline. He grinned and shrugged, then reassumed his earlier cross-legged position. As potential allies, Gundack and Rheemar needed to speak as kren to kren. But to do so, the human would have to sit in his own way. Gundack clicked a command to the young merchant, and the man settled.

"When I close my eyes," Rheemar said, "I keep seeing Jardeen, my sister. She's brushing her night-black hair, the way she did when I last saw her. Her pupils gleam like starstones in sunlight. So beautiful."

The human spoke well, not the way men from isolated villages often did. Gundack grunted to show he listened, that he cared what Rheemar said. Such a tragedy to lose a beloved sister. Or a wife.

"Did you search the pleasure dens of Nath and Blane?" Gundack asked. "Raider krens frequently sell their captives in those port cities." Gundack lifted the tea bowl toward his mouth, bending his short neck down to reach the warm, sweet liquid. "I once rescued a kidnapped krenling in Blane. Not even old enough to know her letters and numbers."

"Let your lips form words of truth."

"Those were the first places I looked," Rheemar said, squinting his hazel eyes. His slender hands tightened around his tea bowl. "The first of a thousand."

Rheemar shifted his body and again rose to a kneeling position, facing Gundack as a fellow kren would. His eyes smoldered, as though his pupils were tea leaves pressed against lumps of charcoal.

"To find Jardeen," Rheemar said, "alive or not, I must find Tarr."

Gundack nodded. This merchant spoke with sincerity. Yet why did Gundack's ears keep tingling? He would propose a plan, then see what he could learn when Rheemar responded.

"Clawkren, whether of desert or mountain tribes, are most vulnerable during the season of sandstorms," Gundack said. "We often sleep for several days at a time. I'm sure you know that. If you find Tarr's winter cave, you can bind him while he sleeps. Amputate his claws. Put out his eyes. Give him no water until you learn where he put your sister."

"I can't hold off until this winter." Rheemar sipped his tea, then placed his bowl on the mat. His upper teeth dug into his lower lip. "Too much time has passed already. I need your help. No one else will do."

"Please elaborate," Gundack said. "I'm not the only kren who seeks to bury Tarr alive."

"Please don't ask me to explain," Rheemar said, his eyes wild, face lit with youthful uncertainty. "Not yet."

Gundack sucked the last of his tea from his bowl with a slurping sound. This conversation was not productive. Only two moon cycles remained until the day of marriages, only three until the season of sandstorms. How could their search of the mountains this year prove fruitful, even if they worked well together?

"You said you didn't know where Tarr is . . . now." A tension spread through Gundack's body. "Might you know where Tarr will find shelter before the sandstorms begin?"

"Perhaps," Rheemar whispered. His gaze darted around the tent, as though he feared someone hid within the shadows. "Yes, I think so."

"You think so?" Gundack clicked, rasped, growled and grunted a string of unflattering remarks. "Why, by the Red Sands, didn't you tell me before?"

"The location of Tarr's cave is dangerous information." Rheemar's voice was unsteady. "Many krens have said you are honorable, but I don't know you. Maybe you would betray me. How can I be sure? We have no pact of loyalty."

"You want a pact?" Gundack flared his nostrils and laughed. "Pacts are made when two warring tribes make a peace agreement. This is not the same situation. There are some odd things called friendship and trust in the Red Desert. Through the years, I've found them quite useful."

"But both take time to develop," Rheemar said. "Would you trust me with your life right now?"

"I know I wouldn't trust your judgment."

"A pact," Rheemar said, "would force the issue."

Did Rheemar have any idea what he was asking? Gundack had been kneeling too long. He stood, then stretched his battle arms above his head. His claws tapped the wooden rod supporting the tent's ceiling. A pact—a blood alliance—with a brother kren was one thing. But between a kren and a human? That could displease the gods. Was this merchant crazy?

"Do you know what will happen," Gundack said, "if our blood runs into each other's veins and something goes wrong with our bodies? We would be better off dying by the claws of Tarr."

"I understand the consequences," Rheemar said, his expression one of small, squeezed eyes and vertical lines between the brows. "Consequences fill my life."

A desert pact. Sealed in front of witnesses. If one lived through the process and later betrayed the trust—even accidentally—the punishment would be a horrific death. The betrayer buried alive in sand, the soul unable to travel to the Cave of Spirit Echoes until the corpse decayed to dust. Ordinary alliances based on family or friendship were better. Each allowed room for mistakes and forgiveness. This pact that Rheemar wanted was better suited to those who were young—and filled with desires to become heroes.

An image of Eutoebi crept into Gundack's mind. Her green and crimson head scales gleamed like polished jewels. Her sensuous spotted lips beckoned him toward her tent and into her four arms. He had no illusions about becoming a hero. He only sought to slay Tarr and soon, then travel to the Mountain of the Dead to obtain Talla's blessing. After that he could make the long journey home to Eutoebi. Honorable actions would be rewarded with an opportunity to again enjoy a loving wife.

"Let us sleep on our thoughts." Gundack rested his friendship hands upon the merchant's shoulders. "And, if a blood alliance is the only solution to both of our dilemmas, we had best pray hard at sunrise."

CHAPTER TWO

A STIRRED POT OF TROUBLE

Twin moons hung in the starry sky. Brother Moon, usually domi-
nant, was a sliver and the sister had waned to quarter-full. Tharda's
star shone like a polished gem. Tharda, the mother of worlds,
always brightened when her youngest children played hiding games.
Gundack would brighten too when Eutoebi bore them children.

Gundack yawned and huddled, side pressed to the ground,
shoulders hunched and knees bent. His tail coiled against his
back. Wait. He was supposed to be on watch. How could he have
let himself drift off to sleep? He pushed his blanket aside, sat up
straight and let the cowl of his cloak slip off his head. His meeting
with the human must have tired him. Such talk of blood pacts.

A pack animal issued a deep guttural rasp. Only Zel's voice had
such a graveled resonance. The eldest sandship lizard in Gundack's
herd of ten rarely growled without good reason. Gundack's ears
flattened and battle arms tensed. His senses explored the chilly
night air the way his father had taught him. Nothing smelled or
sounded wrong.

He dug his claw hands into shallow sand and raised himself to a
squatting position. His back and legs ached. Maybe he was getting
old. Not too old to marry Eutoebi or hunt Tarr. He would never
forget Tarr's massive hands or the yellow tinge to his jagged claws
and triangular head scales. And Tarr had always worn that ring, an

unusually wide band of polished emerald bloodstone. No, he would vanquish Tarr and marry Eutoebi.

Zel growled a little louder. Harness bells tinkled. She moved the short distance to Gundack and nuzzled his shoulder. He stroked the animal's arched neck. Now came a muted shuffling noise, the scrape of sandals against fine chips of rock. Krens never wore sandals. Must be a human. Yet the merchants, both kren and human, who had traveled to Jular Plain should all be asleep in their tents at the base of this plateau. Gundack stood, clicking his tongue in code to signal his back-ups, the brothers Sem and Elar, to intercept the trespasser. Then he moved toward the top of the approach path.

A small ball of light bobbed its way up the incline. Whoever climbed toward this plateau carried a lantern. Kren eyes needed no such assistance in the dark. Human. Who? Not Rheemar? The light disappeared. The trespasser must have ascended to the narrow part of the path and passed between the two towering monoliths of stone, the sentinel rocks.

Gundack shot a quick glance back over his shoulder. The vague silhouettes of his pack animals and caravan drivers remained motionless in the dark. Yet soft grunts and lizard rasps confirmed all had awakened. Gundack sniffed the air for human odors. None. But, then, Zel's foul breath, the product of aging teeth and gums, could overpower weaker smells.

The ball of light appeared again, nearly at the crest of the incline. Gundack could make out a shadowy form beside the approaching lantern. He caught a familiar scent, one he had learned earlier this evening. His tongue clicks instructed Sem and Elar to wait. The merchant man approached.

"Gundack, is that you?" Rheemar's soft, nasal voice sounded apologetic. "Have you thought it over? What I said?"

Thought it over? The merchant had left his tent—come here in the middle of the night—to reopen discussion of a loyalty pact? He should have waited until dawn. The human tapped the uneven ground with his walking stick as he advanced. The lantern in his other hand wobbled back and forth, as though hanging from a lumbering sandship lizard. Had he no good judgment at all?

"Coming to a trader kren's sleeping circle without warning," Gundack said, "is asking to get your throat ripped out." He accented his words with sharp rasps. "I hope you didn't leave valuables unguarded in your tent."

The lamplight softened the appearance of Rheemar's sun-weathered skin. His bearded face appeared younger than before. Not much older than Eutoebi's brother Kan, the day he had left for Nath. Somehow the earlier reading of Rheemar had brought Kan to mind. But Gundack didn't want to think about Kan, and he hadn't for so many moon cycles now. Kan, that coward and traitor, could only prove a distraction.

"I don't think anyone saw me leave," Rheemar said. "I snuffed my candles and didn't light this lantern until I cleared camp. Besides, I put my pack on my sleeping mat and covered it with a blanket. If one of the other merchants pokes his head into my tent, he'll think I'm still there. Now, what about—"

"We'll discuss things later," Gundack said. "At dawn."

"But—" Rheemar said, disappointment on his human face as though Gundack had retracted an offer of hospitality.

"After the sun rises," Gundack said, dismissing the human with the sweep of four hands. "Get some rest."

"How can I sleep?" Rheemar said, his voice changing pitch. "One of the merchants down there is trying to kill me."

"That is a serious accusation." Gundack grunted.

"Don't you believe me?"

Rheemar set down his lantern and extended his arms in an open invitation to be read. Gundack dismissed the gesture with a wave of a battle hand. Merchants were known to overcharge or stretch the truth about the quality of their wares. But murder was not their usual form of treachery. Too many suspicions filled this human's head. Still, if ill feelings brewed down in the encampment, the mood would affect trading. Gundack had already told his caravan drivers what he and Rheemar had discussed this evening. They probably strained to hear this present conversation. He signaled for Sem and the others to come forward.

"These are my tribal kin," Gundack said to Rheemar and introduced his ten companions. "Much passes between us. Nothing travels farther than it should."

"What happened tonight?" Sem said. The brown-striped tip of his tail curled. "What makes you think that anyone but Tarr would bother to kill you?"

Rheemar turned toward Sem, head tilted up, and squinted. Sem's knowledge about him and Tarr probably came as a surprise. A grin spread across Sem's mottled tan and green face, yellowed by lamplight. The inner ends of Rheemar's thick black eyebrows knitted together. The merchant man did not appreciate Gundack's disclosure or Sem's sense of humor. Humans rarely relished the kren practice of candid communication.

Rheemar folded his arms against his chest. Then he rubbed the side of his flat nose. His fingers shifted to his whiskered chin. Finally, he sat on the ground and crossed his legs. Sem crouched on one knee and rested his leathery elbow on the other. Elar did the same, as though they were twins.

"After you left my tent," Rheemar said, "I went to check on my sandship lizard and driver. Then I returned to my tent and fell asleep. I awakened later thirsty. The plug on my water skin wasn't as tight as I had left it."

Gundack knelt in front of Rheemar and grasped his hands. No liar's pulse. And his gaze remained steady. The human projected truth.

"I poured a little water into my cup," Rheemar said. "Touched the surface with the tip of my tongue. It tasted of more than desert wells and goat."

Gundack grunted. Slipping a potion into a goatskin water bag was a well-known trick of murderers and thieves. An unsuspecting victim overlooked the faint bitter taste and, depending on the dose, soon fell into deep or eternal sleep. Rheemar had been clever. But why would one of the merchants want to kill him? Maybe the reason was that this human knew too much of Tarr.

"So you decided," Gundack said, releasing his grip, "it was safer to come up here and risk having your throat slashed by a caravan driver on night watch."

"I guess I sound rather foolish." Rheemar scratched the back of his neck and grinned.

Gundack stood. Most likely, whoever had tampered with Rheemar's water had already discovered he had fled his tent. Little to do about this situation until dawn. They should all go back to sleep. He would stand guard a while longer until Sem took over.

"You'll look as foolish as you sound," Gundack said to Rheemar, "if you try to confront tomorrow with a haggard face and bloodshot eyes."

A shiver traveled through Gundack. Night breezes brought

chilly air. Men had far thinner hides than krens. This one had less body fat than a newborn krenling. Gundack retrieved his blanket and tossed it to Rheemar.

"But, what if an intruder sneaks up here?" Rheemar wrapped the blanket around his shoulders.

"One already tried to," Gundack said. "Don't you remember?"

"This is no time to jest," Rheemar said. "Couldn't someone approach this plateau from an unexpected direction?" He pointed southeast into the night to the cliffs at their back. "What about Jular Steeps?"

"The path you climbed," Gundack said, "is the only way here until daybreak. Believe me. We camp not on a true plateau but a wide ledge that abuts cliffs too sharp and dangerous to descend without daylight."

Gundack took Rheemar's lamp and snuffed out the light. The human truly worried he was in immediate danger. This time, Gundack wouldn't drift off to sleep while on watch. He checked the positions of the moons. His turn to rest would come soon, when Sem assumed guard duty.

§ § §

All slept again in the sleeping circle behind him. Zel's breath filled the breeze. Gundack squatted on the plateau. His eyes studied the darkness. His ears and nose explored the night. No signs of trespassers. Only Rheemar's snores. The human sounded worse than an elderly kren with tongue bloat.

Gundack hadn't camped on Jular Plateau for several years. If treachery simmered in the merchants' encampment, more than one human or kren could be stirring that pot. What if several trekked up here tonight and caused trouble? The approach path branched at one point. The thinner fork led through a maze of boulders that would cause many travelers to lose all sense of direction without the aid of distant reference points. The other approach was the one the human had taken.

But what if trouble came from Jular Steeps, the lofty divided cliff bordering one side of this wide expanse? Gundack stood, stretched, and turned in the general direction of the Steeps, the rugged gateway to the Divider Mountains. Bottomless holes studded that area. Crumbling rocks gave way. No, the route up the back side of that bluff was best climbed in daylight. The vermin who had tampered with Rheemar's water supply had done so tonight. If the traitor brought allies to hunt for the human during the night, they would use the regular approach path, the way Rheemar had. Their advance could be cut off from the side at the point in the path between the boulders.

Cold wind bit into Gundack. He pulled up his cowl, edged back to the sleeping circle and huddled next to Zel. The ground was hard. At least the beast's bulk was a good barricade against rising wind. Gundack rubbed his upper arms. Too bad Zel was cold-blooded and couldn't give off more body heat. Still, sandship lizards were useful traveling companions.

The gods had created both krens and sandship lizards on the same day. Or so the ancient stories claimed. Krens, then cold-blooded creatures, had requested fire to brew tea. The gods had shown them how to kindle fire and steep sugarthorn leaves. That first campfire had warmed krens' blood forever. Gundack wrapped his cloak tighter around his shoulders. Perhaps Zel's ancestors should have asked for fire, too.

Gundack yawned. His eyelids lowered. He forced them open. He must stay awake until Sem took over his duty. Anger would keep him alert. He'd think about Tarr or Kan. Kan. Even Tarr—the wretched son of a pus worm—had never turned against his own blood kin. But Kan had no loyalty, no honor. That thief had betrayed their entire tribe. Gundack's pulse quickened. Yes, thinking of Kan generated enough emotion to keep him awake.

A campfire. How tempting it was to light one and brew sugarthorn tea. But why announce his exact location to potential enemies? Besides, Gundack's father had rarely burned fires after dinner when traveling. Too much smoke clouded sensory perception. The ways of fathers and forefathers should be honored. Gundack inhaled the reek of his pack lizards. Zel's rotting teeth made it difficult enough to detect faint odors. No fire tonight.

Gundack gazed across the plains below. Oh, to stand beside the fragrant cook fire in his tribal encampment. To laugh with his brother-in-law, Robel. To savor the mixed aromas of cragweed tea and smoldering talenbar resin on the annual day of marriages. Eutoebi. To drink in her beauty with all of his senses. To again know the joys and blessings of marriage. Gundack's temples pounded. Even the blood in his vessels desired her.

Gundack inhaled the chilly air. He could almost smell the memory of smoke. Gundack drew a deep breath. Wait. Smoke. This was no recollection. The aroma of a dying cook fire must have wafted from the merchants' encampment below. But this odor wasn't from burning wood. More like hides. The harness bells of sandship lizards tinkled. He sat up straight and clicked a warning to Sem and the others.

Gundack moved over smooth stones toward the open edge of the plateau. The area bordering this cliff held treacherous holes, deep and wide enough to trap a kren. A dense groundcover of creeping mountain sugarthorn covered the bores. With each step, his toes tested the ground until he had ventured far enough to survey the merchants' encampment.

Darkness engulfed the tents. Yet a cylinder of light flickered down there. The light appeared central to the camp, inside or near the merchant men's area. But the cooking circle had been within the kren section. This illumination fanned outward and leaped into the night. Gundack's ears flattened. Tents were on fire.

CHAPTER THREE

AS THOUGH THE AIR BURNED

"Fire," Gundack rasped. "Tents ablaze in the merchants' encampment."

The palm of his claw hand pushed against Rheemar's shoulder. The sleeping human mumbled and twitched one hand, as though brushing away an insect. Gundack shook him harder. Rheemar roused, groggy and eyes half-closed.

"Your camp's on fire." Gundack slapped the human's cheek with his friendship hand. "Fire. In the tents below."

"My gods." The human scrambled and groped for his lantern. "We've got to go down there. We've got to warn people. Warn krens. Do something."

"Hides don't burn well. This fire spreads too fast." Gundack raised himself to standing. "Fire resin. Some fool must have left a burning candle near a sack of flammable resin."

Why weren't the merchants' sandship lizards roaring the alarm from the opposite side of the encampment? Gundack had seen twenty or thirty of the beasts this afternoon. Another sound, a distant cry, iced his blood. A neglected candle hadn't started this fire. The encampment was under attack.

"Prepare to defend," Gundack called.

"What are you talking about?" Rheemar said and stood motionless.

"Don't you hear it yet?" Gundack clutched Rheemar's arm.

"Hear what?" Rheemar said. The human blinked several times, with a rapid jerky motion.

"Those distant roars," Gundack said. "Raider krens."

Raider krens rarely launched attacks at daybreak and never in the middle of the night. Why now? Would they limit their onslaught to the merchant's camp? Or advance to this plateau? What were they after?

Drivers stumbled here and there in the darkness. They clicked their tongues and prodded sandship lizards. The beasts growled, yet no harness bells tinkled. The animals weren't moving into the necessary semi-circular defense formation. They weren't moving at all. Wind chilled Gundack's face and cut through his cloak, robe and tunic. Neither a campfire nor sunshine warmed their cold-blooded muscles. That was the problem. The sandships had gotten too cold.

"Zel," Gundack clicked, "get the other sandships into position."

Zel had better do her job as lead pack animal. And fast. The lizards, with their heavy jaws and long rows of sharp teeth, must face the approach path. Gundack slapped Zel's rump with the back of his claw hand. Zel rasped an anxious growl.

"Where can you use me best?" Rheemar asked.

His hazy outline included his walking stick. He leaned on his spade staff as though his legs might buckle. Did a potion muddle his mind? What about that tainted water he had tasted at the encampment? No sounds, no screams of pain or terror came from the merchants' camp. Only the war cries of raiders. Gundack's ears flattened against the top of his head. A traitor must have added a sleeping potion to all of the merchants' water supplies. No one inside the tents would escape.

"Go where you won't fall down a hole," Gundack said, "or get slashed to shreds."

"I can do something to help." Rheemar tapped the spade end of his staff. "And I've got a hand sling."

A sling? The weapon of human farmers and herdsmen was good at a distance in daylight, not at quarter moons in the dark. Besides, human eyes didn't work well while the sun slept. This human was no better than cold and lethargic sandship lizards.

"If you want to help," Gundack said, "stay with the sandships. Rub their legs to get them warm."

"You don't understand," Rheemar said. "I'm really good with a sling."

"You're the one who doesn't understand," Gundack said and turned toward Jular Plain.

"But," Rheemar said. The human tugged on the bottom of Gundack's cloak.

Why was this human so uncooperative? Gundack growled a throaty warning. Rheemar jumped backward, his black eyebrows pulled a third of the way up his forehead, as though strings controlled them. Maybe now he'd do as told.

Gundack stared into the night. Flames rose from all of the central tents and spread. Fire would destroy the rugs, the woven robes, the perishable valuables the merchants had brought. What reward would the invaders gain? Then Gundack's mind whispered the answer to his own question.

"They've come for you," Gundack said. He reached out and pressed the palm of his claw hand against Rheemar's cool shoulder.

"Tarr." Rheemar's voice quavered.

"Tarr's krens." Gundack scanned the blackness. "I doubt Tarr would give us the pleasure of his company."

Rheemar knew Tarr's secret. If he died before revealing it,

Gundack could not avenge Talla this year. Maybe not ever. There had to be a place to conceal the human and sequester his odor.

"Go to the base of the Steeps," Gundack said to Rheemar. "Follow the cliff to the far end of this plateau. Find a cave or the cavity in a large boulder."

"You wouldn't climb behind a rock like a coward," Rheemar said. "Why should I?"

Why couldn't this human do as he was told? Gundack needed to focus on a defense strategy. Distant crackles of fire intensified. The smell of burning hides did, too.

How had the raiders approached the merchants' encampment without pack lizards detecting them? Gundack's own beasts would have filled the night with roars. Unless the kren who had poisoned the water and started the fire had been a trusted driver already in the camp. The traitorous driver could have fed merchants and sand-ships a potion. Then set fire with resin and lamp oil. Yes, it must have happened that way.

But, what was this? Gundack stared down from the plateau and blinked. Balls of flames moved beyond the central conflagration, floating like spirits through the air. Raider krens, holding torches, moving out of the merchants' encampment.

"They're headed this way," Rheemar said and moved toward the edge of the plateau.

"Stay clear of the sugarthorn," Gundack said. "That's where holes plunge to the ancient caverns. You'll fall into one. Stand back."

"I'll be fine," Rheemar said.

Would he? Gundack strained to count the number of torches. More than fifteen. Maybe twenty. Twenty would make too small a group for raider krens. Forty to eighty would be more likely.

Probably half to three-quarters of the warriors carried spears instead of torches. How many carried metal or leather shields? Spears and shields would make them formidable foes, day or night. Gundack's krens had daggers, and only a few spears and the usual walking sticks tipped with trenching spades.

"Gather every weapon we've got," Gundack called to Sem and turned toward Rheemar. "Come this way."

"I'm thinking," Rheemar said.

"Then think in a safer place." Gundack had wasted enough time on Rheemar. "Come."

The tinkle of harness bells multiplied in the darkness—the beautiful, uneven rhythm of ten lethargic sandship lizards consenting to stand and form their defense line. Metal objects clinked and webbed feet shuffled. Drivers removed spears and spades from their packs. They dragged mats and supplies behind the line of sandship lizards in the dark to protect possessions from torches.

Could anything else be set afire? Jular Plateau was treeless. Bushes grew only on one side, against the base of the Steeps. Mountain sugarthorn was thick along the plateau's open edge and sparse everywhere else. Little more than packs and living flesh could be set ablaze.

Gundack groped through his own pack and found his two silver daggers. He tossed off his cloak, then strung both knife sheaths on the sash of his thigh-length robe. Krens did close combat with their claw hands alone. Mountain krens were smaller than their desert counterparts. Most raiders were mountain dwellers. Their dull-colored head scales absorbed less of Father Sun's divine energy. Two to three would rush Gundack at once. A well-aimed dagger would bring one down.

Torches below brightened and appeared to reshape. The raiders had cleared the encampment and changed direction. They chanted in unison. Too far away to decipher the words. The translucent membranes protecting Gundack's pupils slid toward the corners of his eyes. He focused on the torchlight, as though the flaring represented a giant pulse, a life force. Now, he could almost see the raiders' claws sharpened for the kill. He could almost hear their webbed claw feet pound the ground.

Gundack's group would be outnumbered, even if all their knives and spears hit the attackers. Trenching spades might slow down a few more. Rotten odds at best. The raiders advanced cloaked in blackness toward the base of an incline and the trail leading to Gundack and his krens. Sem's deep voice rasped out another order. More dragging sounds followed. All of the supplies must be behind the lizards by now. Gundack needed a more comprehensive strategy. What would work best? Or, at all? It was time to assign defense stations.

§ § §

An uneven line of fiery torches cut through the darkness on the plain below, as though the air burned. Raiders headed for the plateau and Gundack's encampment. He must hold them back. He signaled for Sem to kneel beside him on the stony ground. Rheemar joined him, too.

"I've got an idea," Rheemar said. "We need to divide into two groups. One unit should stay here and warm the sandships so they can fight. The rest need to go where they can slow the raiders' advance."

"The raiders will be the most vulnerable," Sem said, his eyes fixed on Gundack, "when they climb the approach path."

Sem slid the back of one claw finger across his moonlit throat.

Gundack grunted. Sem's advice always was valuable, and Rheemar's suggestion actually sounded reasonable. Maybe the human had seen battle before, despite his young age.

"Let me think," Gundack said.

Gundack had used one battle arm for stability when he had returned from Rheemar's tent and climbed the steep, uneven path. Raider krens would do the same. Their friendship hands would hold their shields. Friendship arms could not reach and protect all vital parts of a kren's frame. Ascending the trail would make those mountain vermin susceptible targets. Gundack and his drivers must strike while the raiders climbed.

"Yes." Gundack rose, took a deep breath, and motioned to the others. "The path narrows where it winds between the sentinel stones. A good place for an ambush."

The gods had once promised that desert clawkren would rule the Red Sands forever. Yet he stood near the passage to the Divider Mountains, far from his desert home, far from ancestral Red Sands. He might not have the right to ask the gods for this victory. Once a soothsayer had predicted that Gundack would call forth a hero. Surely now was the time for an ancient hero. A prayer to the one who had rescued Father Sun might be appropriate. Gundack would invoke Talla's spirit, as well.

Now for the weapons. He had two daggers. Rheemar had only a spade staff and sling. The human had refused to hide from Tarr's krens and would need something more. Gundack loosened his sash and stepped closer to the merchant.

"My father purchased my knives in the northlands." Gundack handed Rheemar a sheathed dagger, hilt end first. "This might bring good luck."

"Thank you," Rheemar said, chin tilted upward. "I believe I was meant to be here tonight. If I hadn't noticed that someone

"Then tonight," Rheemar said, "I'll fight for the desert."

had tampered with my water skin . . . " He threaded his waist sash through the top of the knife sheath, then bowed his head.

"My father," Gundack said, "slept beside his sandship lizards and drivers on every trading journey. He chose safe places to spend each night. If not for his teachings, I would have slept in a tent tonight or bedded down my lizards with those of the merchants." He re-knotted his sash around his waist. "The old ways—desert ways—are best."

"Then tonight," Rheemar said, "I'll fight for the desert."

A lofty idea. More likely the human would fight for his life. Gundack moved toward the sandship lizards and clicked his tongue. His tribal kin gathered in front of Zel. Pale moonlight textured Rheemar's face. The hexagonal head scales of the drivers appeared bordered with gold. Attackers' claws might soon bloody them all.

"Hold the raiders on the incline of the approach path," Gundack said, his voice low. "Sem, you and your cousin cover one of the sentinel stones. Elar and I will take the other. Position your three brothers-in-law up the incline."

"If they get past you," the eldest brother-in-law said, "they won't escape us."

"The rest of you—including Rheemar—stay with the sandships," Gundack said.

"What if," Rheemar said, "some of the raiders actually evade all of us? They could double back to the sentinels and get you from behind." Rheemar was now a disembodied voice in the night. "What if they reach us before the lizards are ready?"

"Then we had all better pray," Sem said with deep rasps, "that the sun rises early and our sandships fight well."

Spear in hand, Gundack edged from the plateau down the approach path. Feet crunched gravel behind him as the others moved toward their assigned positions. He mounted a broad, flat rock, shifting his tail for balance. This formation would lead to one of the monoliths. He reached up, felt the smooth rock face, and set his spear in a long, high crevice. His claws dug into cracks. He scaled upward, edged the spear to the next level and pulled himself higher. Could the raiders hear his movements? No, they would still be too far away. But he could hear them.

"Death to our foes," a raider called.

"Victory to Tarr," another said.

Between the words came the crackle of torches flaring, followed by the smell of burning pitch and the reek of their bodies. Stinkwood, their cooking oil, fouled breath and sweat. Gundack could see their shifting light again. The first line of raiders had reached the turn, halfway up the incline. They would ascend to the narrows next.

Gundack crawled onto flat stone, the surface smooth as new glass. He had reached one of the sentinel formations. He crouched near the monolith and panted, detecting the odor of kren and human blood. Dead merchants. Blood had spilled onto murderous claws and dried by the heat of fire.

Gundack reached for his amulet. Of course it wasn't there. Why had he done that? Kan had stolen the silver charm two years ago, then fled the desert. Only a coward would have run away. Gundack might die tonight while defending himself and his friends. Yet death with honor would be better than any life Kan must lead.

Gundack gripped his silver dagger. May desert krens rule the Red Sands forever. His eyelids raised high, allowing translucent membranes to part. May he live to father krenlings with Eutoebi. His pupils focused. May they together continue their family lines. His arms prepared to strike. Surely the gods would forgive him for praying with open eyes and an unbowed head.

CHAPTER FOUR

AN APPROPRIATE GREETING

Torchlight flickered in the darkness. The odor of mountain krens grew strong, smelling like putrid fat on a hot day. Gundack stood atop the high foundation stone of the taller monolith, his back pressed against cold, smooth rock. Tarr's advance guards would be in range soon. Tension curled Gundack's tail into a tight coil. He clasped the hilt of his silver dagger and inhaled short, quiet breaths. Surely Sem had reached the sentinel stone on the opposite side of the path. Gundack did not dare step from his hiding place to check. Raiders might detect him. There would be little time to select his target and aim, even less time to hurl the knife downward. He must hold the blade just right.

"Death to the desert krens," voices said. "Victory to Tarr."

The chants of the raiders rose. These advance guards knew they would be the first in line to face knives, spears and slashing claws. They sounded confident. Did they believe their numbers protected them? Perhaps they feared what Tarr could do to their families. Gundack fingered the cold knife. Yellow torchlight illuminated the rock to his right. His skin tingled. Now was the moment. He stepped from behind the sentinel. The hazy outline of a raider kren's back passed below. Gundack launched his knife on its journey. The thief lurched forward and groaned. Gundack moved back behind the monolith.

"The vermin got my brother," a kren shouted.

"Ambush," another said.

Feet scuffled in loose dirt and gravel. A weapon meant for Gundack clanked against nearby stone. A clatter of wood and metal reverberated, as though hailstones pelted a metal bowl. Gundack pressed his back against a recess of curved rock. His muscles tensed. The base of his tail throbbed. Torchlight swelled. Then the pained cry of a kren pierced the night, and a yellow light disappeared. Sem. He must have felled a torchbearer.

"I'll rip out your hearts," a mountain kren shouted.

No. Sem's three brothers-in-law would do the ripping. Gundack moistened his lips. The owner of that voice would soon encounter claws. Now he needed additional weapons. He heard tapping from his left, five raps of a claw against rock. A desert kren's signal. Gundack reached into the darkness and fingered several elongated wooden shafts. Elar had retrieved the raiders' errant spears and set them on top of the foundation boulder. All was going well. Another pool of light illuminated the far edge of the monolith. Feet crunched gravel. More of Tarr's krens approached, no longer chanting.

The odor of stinkwood oil again became strong. Gundack grasped one of the spears. The wooden shaft felt rough in his hand. He stepped from behind the monolith, hurled the weapon and leaped back to safety. Spear tips clattered against nearby rock. He smelled blood. His ears rose. The night brought a medley of throaty rasps and gurgles. He had hit a raider in the windpipe.

A ragged hue edged the night. A hazy, pale pink streak lined the horizon. Dawn approached. Dawn would bring the sun to warm his lizards. Yet it would also permit some of the raiders to climb the back side of Jular Steeps and attack Gundack's camp from a second direction. How many of the enemy remained? At least six or seven had passed by already. Seventy or more krens might be massed on this path. But the odor did not seem strong enough for seventy. Because of shifting wind direction? No, they had already divided their force, sending many to the Steeps.

Yellow light swelled. He grasped another spear and bent his raised battle arm, clenched claw hand angled back over his shoulder. Bright illumination stung his eyes and surrounded the bearer with haze. His protective membranes closed, then he launched the spear. A weapon sped by Gundack, less than an arm's length away. He ducked behind the monolith. That had been close. He must move faster next time.

His ears searched for sounds. Nothing. The raiders knew where he and Sem waited and were holding their positions. Yes, with hazy daylight lining the horizon, most of Tarr's krens would be working their way toward the Steeps. Time for Elar to take charge of Gundack's defense post.

Gundack clicked a signal. A shadowy outline of two claw hands gripped a sheltered section of the foundation's narrow table. Elar's thick battle arms pulled him upward and onto the ledge. Early daylight framed Elar's broad face and gave his crimson and green head scales a polished luster. Gundack clasped Elar's friendship hands and felt the warmth of loyalty. The driver's golden eyes smoldered with hate for Tarr's krens.

"It's a stand-off here," Gundack said, with soft clicks and rasps. "Hold back those sons of pus worms if they try to advance. I'm heading for the Steeps."

Gundack lowered himself down the back side of the foundation boulder, his chest against rock. His toes found a niche, and he shifted his weight. Sem also would have ordered another comrade to cover his post. He and Sem needed to make their way to the cliffs together. Gundack's ears flattened. He pointed them upward to hear. A soft, distant growl increased in intensity. Growls turned to roars. Gundack's sandship lizards sounded the alarm. The first of Tarr's krens must have reached the crest of Jular Steeps, readying themselves for the downward swoop to Gundack's camp. Cold air numbed Gundack's friendship hands. It was still so early. Zel's legs would remain lethargic until after the sun fully rose. Gundack and his drivers must thwart the attackers.

All of the sandship lizards bellowed now, each one trying to sound more menacing than the others. Zel probably had prodded the other lizards into a semicircle by now, a deadly wall of teeth and claws. Fine gravel scratched the webbing between Gundack's toes. He had reached the bottom of the monolith's foundation. Those animals had vulnerable throats, though. A strong throwing arm with a spear could bring a sandship lizard down. He ran down a side path toward the echoing din. Gundack needed to strike while the thieves descended Jular Steeps, but he had no spear or dagger.

Gundack scrambled over uneven rocks, his tail shifting, then he squeezed through a narrow passageway between boulders. Gritty dust coated his mouth. Saliva dripped on his robe and wet the top of his tunic underneath. All manner of weapons were now scarce. Earlier, he had prayed for victory. He should have prayed for a landquake. He headed up an incline. A clicking noise came from behind him. He stopped and wheeled around, battle arms spread wide. A familiar kren with hexagonal red and green head scales and thin spotted lips grinned. Sem.

"There are clumps of brush," Sem said. He panted hard. "At the bottom of the Steeps. We've got to set them afire."

The Steeps had two side-by-side bluffs, joined from their bases to their halfway points. Both cliffs towered over the terrain, though one stood a little shorter. Wait. Didn't blue cragweed thrive in crevices above the split between the two cliffs? Gundack's tongue rimmed his lips. Where cragweed did well, golden mottleflower could usually be found. Smoke from burning mottleflower was potent enough to confuse minds and bodies, make eyes see strange things. What an appropriate way to greet Tarr's krens as they crawled on their bellies down Jular Steeps.

"We must ignite the crevice weeds," Gundack said, an arm's length behind Sem, "as well as the bottom brush. If I can approach the ledge line from the side with a torch, wind will carry the flames along. I will hold my breath once patches of cragweed ignite. Long enough to escape the mottleflower smoke."

"Could Rheemar help?" Early morning sun glistened on Sem's crusty head scales.

"Maybe."

Gundack edged between more tall boulders, continuing toward the Steeps. Pink streaks lined the sky. Something about Rheemar tickled his mind. A thought he couldn't reach. Rheemar had left his tent in the middle of the night and come to their sleeping circle without warning. A dangerous thing to do. He had asked for a loyalty pact, then claimed a merchant had tried to poison him. Might he somehow have learned about the planned burning of the encampment? Had he escaped to save his own hide? Had he then been horrified upon seeing the camp ablaze?

Or the human's actions could have been less innocent. Tarr often gained cooperation through coercion. His krens could have threatened to kill Rheemar's sister if he didn't arrange the fire. A sick feeling washed through Gundack. Rheemar might know the location of Tarr's winter hiding cave because the two were allies.

Rheemar might have come to Gundack's camp to betray him to the raiders.

Gundack emerged from the passageway between boulders and looked up to the towering blackened stone faces of the Steeps to his left. Spires of jagged rock bordered the Steeps' flat cliff-tops, like spines on a lizard bird's head. Figures wearing yellow and brown robes stood behind some of those spires. Already mountain krens—Tarr's krens—controlled the nearest cliff of the Steeps. Did Rheemar lie in wait for Gundack and his drivers at the base of that promontory?

Sem clicked his tongue and crouched in dawn's shadows. Gundack dropped to his hands and knees and moved beside him. Wind fluttered the edges of Sem's linen robe. Irregular furrows lined his blotchy tan and pale green face.

"What bothers you?" Sem asked.

"Rheemar," Gundack said. "If hidden truths can nip at an ankle, they are apt to also leap for the throat."

"How fast can you get that mottleflower burning?" Sem asked.

Sem had caught on to his idea. Tarr's krens might do so, too. Yet he and Sem had to try something. Gundack grunted.

CHAPTER FIVE

PREPARE TO DIE

Saliva dripped from Gundack's tongue. His bare feet pounded the barren stretch of plateau toward Zel and the other sandship lizards. Sweat wet his chest and belly skin. He matched Sem's frantic pace across stone-studded ground. Cold wind hit his cheeks, a welcome relief. Ahead, Zel's scarlet and green head plates glistened, like kettleplant leaves wet with dew. The gods had created desert krens to tend to the daily needs of sandship lizards. Caravan leaders and drivers had fulfilled this role for countless generations. In turn the large beasts fought beside their krens in battle. Loyalty flowed in the veins of both beings. Zel bellowed a comrade's war call to Gundack.

The pack animals stood in a semicircle in the middle of the plateau, their heads facing outward and stomachs close to the ground. Zel arched her long, scaly neck and roared an anxious greeting. The beast's spiked, green tail drummed dirt and fine gravel. Her squat legs, knees bent at right angles to her elongated body, rocked. Big lizards had pulled the gods' mighty ships through deserts before the red dunes had formed. Zel looked as majestic as her ancestors must have been. She would be battle-ready on time. How good to inhale her foul breath and taste the air's rancid flavor. Gundack's father had raised this animal. A friend was a friend.

Sem clicked instructions to the waiting drivers and grabbed a lantern, barely breaking stride. He panted hard and dashed toward the shorter black cliff of the Steeps, the one Tarr's krens controlled.

"Give me your torch," Gundack said to the nearest driver. "If Zel's blood needs more warming, you'll have to rub her legs."

Gundack hurried after Sem, holding the burning torch high. The oily odor of pitch smoke filled his nostrils. His side ached and chest heaved hard. The soles of his feet stung. He needed to stop and catch his breath, but there wasn't time.

More raiders gathered on top of the Steeps. How lusterless these krens' head scales were, almost devoid of green pigmentation. Even the reds appeared faded. One raider carried something heavy. Gundack opened his eye membranes. Wind tossed sand into one eye. He blinked until the stinging subsided and the membranes slid back to a half-open position. Now he could see the raider and the prize he carried. The kren had a rope anchor. These vermin would descend faster using lines.

Raiders bellowed death threats from the cliff above and secured several ropes with sets of sturdy iron hooks. They would maneuver well on their descent, far better than they could if crawling or with a grapnel line. Cloth covered their mouths and noses. Tarr's krens not only expected fire, they had prepared to pass through smoke and swing clear of flames as they neared the ground. But had they anticipated burning mottleflower? Still, there were so many. Gundack's ears flattened against his head and the base of his tail throbbed. The skirmish at the narrows had been nothing. The real battle gathered ahead, like an approaching sandstorm.

୧ ୧ ୧

Dew still coated the morning. Sem thrust the lantern into brush and set the first clump ablaze. The fire took hold far faster than Gundack had expected. Flames crackled louder than an angry old kreness could click her tongue. The gods must have wanted this.

The heat of the fire didn't reach Gundack. Brush was sparse near the approach to his climb. These flames would not jump to his robe or tunic now. Still, a shifting wind would send unwanted smoke in his direction. And Tarr's krens would descend the ropes soon. He must reach the cragweed and accomplish his task while conditions remained favorable. Gundack edged up a steep cut in the rock face. He hugged the cliff, each step a new challenge. The chilly morning air carried the war chants of raider krens, yet no spears flew in his direction. Probably the angle was wrong, and the raiders wouldn't waste their efforts or weapons.

He moved higher. The odor of burning leaves and thorns blended with the oily scent of his torch. The curve of his path led him above a section of the thicket fire. Heat warmed his torch arm. A shower of cinders landed on a ledge below. Gundack could still accomplish his task and remain unscorched, as long as the wind didn't shift and gust.

The shelf he climbed tapered, no longer wide enough for both feet and became nearly vertical. He could never scale straight up the Steeps with a torch unless rope dangled from above. If the gods wanted mottleflower to burn and confuse Tarr's krens, they would have to show him a better way to reach the cragweed. To continue facing forward, he would have to shuffle upward with one foot, then drag the rear one into place, heel to toe. Shifting wind pushed against his back. Gundack gripped the cliff tighter with his friendship hand and the claws on his fingers and toes. Loose rocks crumbled in his grasp. The shelf disappeared into the cliff. He could go no farther. Time to change his strategy.

Ragged lines of cragweed grew below the largest one he had hoped to reach. If he started the fire on the lowest line, flames might jump to higher levels. He stood on his claw toes and angled his extended torch arm over his head, reaching for the bed of crag-weed. The plants caught, probably the dried undergrowth. The gods of wind and fire—and perhaps Talla's spirit—were giving him a chance.

A whirring, nearly hidden by roars, rasps and growls, made his ears perk and tilt upward. The sound, intermittent, cut through the air. Gundack glanced up. Pointed blue-green blades of cragweed overhung a ledge that blocked his view. The whirring came from behind him. Behind, and above, too. He had heard that sound before, yet not in battle. Still the sound brought no clear image or meaning to mind. And his attention needed to stay with the task at hand.

Wind fanned the flames along the line of cragweed. The roars of krens swelled. He couldn't focus on what was happening up the cliff. He had to get away from the fire and smoke before mottle-flower in the deeper recesses ignited. Mottleflower never affected judgment, sight or balance immediately. But he didn't know how much delay or impairment would occur after he inhaled the plant's smoke.

He edged backward, the hands on his right side gripping the cliff. But he wasn't moving fast enough and couldn't see where he placed his feet. He hurled the torch downward, then faced the cliff. Brush smoke grew strong. He coughed. The wind probably had changed direction. Now the smoke carried a sweet and spicy odor, a smell his father had once described. Burning mottleflower.

Gundack shut his mouth and nostrils. He skidded sideways down the shelf, his feet and four hands scrambling against crum-bling rock. His tail thrashed this way and that. His feet found wider footholds. He took steps now, no longer sliding. Then the surface became smooth, stable rock. He had reached the lower half of the climb. He leaped from the shelf, arms and legs spread, and landed with a thud on the plateau. Oh, how his chest ached for air.

Pain raced up his spine. A spasm rose in his chest. He coughed as though his lungs turned inside out. Certainly the raiders must be on their way down the cliff by now. And there was that humming noise again. He whipped around and faced the opposite direction.

A lone figure stood near the edge of the right cliff, the higher one. Rheemar. There he stood, legs apart and knees flexed, his head turned to the side in line with his outstretched arm. Rheemar curved his other arm and worked a hand sling. The weapon hummed, cut a broad circle through the air and launched a stone across the rift between cliffs toward the opposite side. The human's black braids shifted with his body's forward thrust. Even as the rock hit a kren in the throat, Rheemar whirled the next stone and another.

A kren staggered on the shorter cliff. Another dropped to his knees. A third fell off the top of a climbing rope and plunged to the burning thicket. Rheemar had such deadly accuracy and power. Gundack had seen herdsmen work slings, but not with Rheemar's strength and coordination. He stood alone on the equivalent of an island in the air. The only way to reach the table was to scale the cliff's steep face, the way he must have done. Raiders threw few spears in Rheemar's direction. He was beyond their range of accuracy. Tarr's krens took cover behind boulders and rock spires.

But a dozen raiders mounted ropes. The thieves slid downward, legs wrapped around the lines. They pushed their feet against the rock face and swung outward, past the rim of burning cragweed. They would reach the ground in mere moments. Rheemar could not pelt them all. Gundack signaled his krens to prepare for hand-to-hand combat.

How many of Tarr's krens had come here? Would the thieves

have inhaled any of the smoke from burning mottleflower? How many had Rheemar hit? Gundack could see figures—maybe twelve or so—slumped above on the Steeps. Some moved. Some didn't. Rheemar had felled a few on the climbing ropes. Close to forty remained in fighting condition. Five of Gundack's krens were still at the narrows. That left five others plus himself. Yet Gundack had Rheemar on his side. At least, until the human ran out of stones. Maybe the sandship lizards would have warmed up enough then to join the battle.

He filled his lungs with air and exhaled. Several raiders pushed off the rock face, swung over the burning thicket and released the ropes. The krens landed upright, feet thudding against gravel-coated ground. One charged in his direction. The rest headed towards his drivers or the base of Rheemar's cliff. Oh, to lick Eutoebi's spotted lips one more time. To explore the irregular texture of her delicate pointed ears. May bravery rule his heart this day. What would come, would come. Gundack pulled himself to his full height and roared his battle cry.

Another call trumpeted from behind him and echoed off the Steeps. Harness bells tinkled with a steady rhythm. Zel. Gundack turned his head. His pack animals waddled, their arched necks bobbing forward and back with each lumbering step. Their curled lips exposed sharp gray teeth. The sandship lizards had no speed yet, but they were on their way.

Another horde of raiders swung off their ropes and landed. Gundack dodged an on-coming raider's claws, veered, and slashed flesh. Blood flowed from the kren's belly, and he doubled over with a howl. Gundack glanced to the left. Sem clutched one shoulder with his friendship hand, chestnut blood seeping through his fingers. His claws tore into a staggering opponent. Zel's jaws crunched the back of the disoriented raider's neck. Lizards roared and trampled assailants in their path. Surely Gundack's five drivers at the narrows could hear the sounds of battle. Would they try to return to the plateau? If they did, Tarr's other krens would join the main battle, too.

Rheemar still worked a sling atop his cliff. But several raiders crawled up the rock face to overtake him. How foolish Gundack had been to think Rheemar might be Tarr's ally. If only he could help the human now. But the next round of assailants sped toward Gundack and more swung off the ropes. Few flames shot from the thicket, and the cragweed fire up the cliff had burned itself out. The next attackers would not be poisoned by mottleflower.

"Prepare to die," a raider with yellow eyes bellowed. His red, green and brown coloration looked as dull as old pottery covered with dust. Two of his comrades followed close behind. All had deep notches in their ears. Mountain kren.

The vermin lunged toward Gundack, his breath hot and foul. His claw hand ripped though the air with a broad sweeping motion. Gundack jerked backward. Claws swiped toward his belly. Gundack dodged again, using his arm for a shield. Claws tore into his left wrist, then his forearm. Pain shot to his shoulder. Bright chestnut blood pulsed from his gaping wounds. He thrust his body forward, aimed for the raider's eye, and instead dug his other set of claws into his assailant's cheek. Gundack's timing was off. Still the raider roared and pressed the heel of his claw hand against his wounded face.

Blood streamed down Gundack's left arm and drenched the front of his robe. His vision blurred. How much blood was he losing? Would he sink to his knees and became unconscious? The two other krens—one with large green blotches on his forehead—moved in an arc, out of Gundack's reach. Their tactic was clear—slash him from behind.

Gundack cradled his bleeding arm against his stomach. His friendship hands pressed hard on the jagged wounds. He leaped backward to escape another thrust of claws, then sideways. These two closed in fast. He had to slash at least one of them in the throat. Gundack braced for the next blast of pain. It didn't come.

Instead a tall, brawny raider approached Gundack. He was larger than most mountain krens with deep notches in his ears. His feet pounded the ground like thunder gods drumming in the sky. His spotted lips curled in a snarl. Gundack noticed something odd about the kren, something he couldn't quite define. Maybe the way the raider shifted his body while running. Or the yellow tinge to his triangular red and green head scales. Or his monstrous hands and yellow claws. A questioning glare settled into the raider's face, as though he too fought to dredge up a memory. Then his yellow eyes exuded hate and contempt.

"Gundack of the Red Sands," the raider bellowed. "Prepare to join Talla."

The raider raised one arm. A wide green band with amber and red-brown flecks rested around the raider's first claw finger, the ring a polished emerald bloodstone. Gundack's ears flattened against his head. This kren was Tarr.

CHAPTER SIX

LAST MOMENT ALIVE

Tarr's yellow eyes mocked Gundack. Yellow claws prepared to shred his throat. Lusterless brown blotches spotted his flat nose and cheekbones. Wind rippled his short black robe. A guttural roar poured out of him, as though he tried to make the Divider Mountains tremble.

"This is your last morning of life," Tarr said.

Gundack's own pulse vibrated and pounded. Vermin. Tarr had murdered Talla. He had ripped away the serenity of Gundack's life and filled the raw wounds in his once-peaceful soul with relentless hate. And Tarr had ignited all those merchants in the encampment, taken them from their families. Yet how would Gundack beat this son of a pus worm? How would he survive and marry Eutoebi? Gundack's chestnut blood stained his own robe and skin. His injured left battle arm throbbed with pain. Sem and the other driver krens were fighting for their own lives. Tarr had brought misery to too many. The time for vengeance had arrived.

"No," Gundack said. "This is your first day of death."

He had more to say but floating visions filled his mind. The upturned face of a kreness, golden eyes brimming with love. Tiny pale fingers grasping a scarred green and brown hand. Images again broke Gundack's concentration. Were the gods bringing him visions? Had they blown mottleflower smoke into his face so he could touch Tarr's thoughts? Maybe the gods were directing him to use his transcendent abilities to his advantage. Chestnut and gray hues swirled, spilled blood of Sem glistening on stones. If Gundack fell in battle, raiders would slaughter Sem and the others, confiscate goods his tribe needed to survive. That mustn't happen. Maybe he could use customs and visions to protect all he cherished.

"No," Gundack shouted. "This is not the time of death for my comrades or any more of yours. Withdraw your krens and I'll withdraw mine. I demand satisfaction according to the laws of all desert and mountain tribes. This fight must be between the two of us. No retribution for the outcome. No spoils."

Tarr scowled, leathery skin crinkling around the corners of his mouth and eyes. He straightened, battle arm on his hip and legs parted. Tarr would lose honor if he denied Gundack. Yet many mountain krens had little honor to lose.

"We want the human," Tarr rasped.

"He became our traveling companion," Gundack said, "before you attacked. Custom mandates loyalty to traveling companions until the journey ends."

Tarr issued another piercing roar and flattened his notch ears against his triangular head scales. A white figure, a krenling of chalk, appeared in Gundack's thoughts, then vanished. Another vision from Tarr's mind. How odd to think of a slave or helper wife at a time such as this.

"You expect me to agree?" Tarr bellowed a laugh. "You really think I'd do that? I, the chosen of the God of Thieves, the warrior whose seed will save my tribe?"

Stacks of linen robes flickered within Gundack's mind. Images of thick woven carpets swelled and faded. Tarr's thoughts again. Tarr had reaped no plunder from the merchants' encampment. He wanted the riches Gundack's caravan carried—as well as the human who knew too much about him.

"Even the God of Thieves," Gundack said, "expects you to agree. Does he have more honor than you?"

"Then I'll fight and kill only you," Tarr said. "But I'll claim the human and whatever possessions I choose."

The raiders would spare the lives of Sem and Gundack's other drivers. They would take everything and leave nothing but his tribal kin alive. Not good enough, but a start.

ʕ ʕ ʕ

Jular Steeps towered behind the wide ledge of Jular Plateau. Sem, Zel and the rest of Gundack's drivers stood together with Rheemar. Tarr's raiders gathered to their right, shoulder to shoulder in a line. Gundack moved away from these spectators and on toward the brink of the plateau and Jular Plain below. Tarr walked up and stood almost close enough to touch Gundack. He would make the first move. Tribal laws gave the raider that right.

Gundack was no warrior. He must remain upright and out of Tarr's reach if he were to survive. Fear and determination washed through him in equal proportions. He would wait for opportunity to strike. All he needed was one moment, one misjudgment by Tarr and a prompting vision. He parted his legs and arched his uninjured battle arm. Precise movements were nearly impossible with only one battle arm. If he was worthy, Tharda would give him all that he needed.

Tarr lunged, his curved claws slashing through air at Gundack's face. Gundack leaped backward, his good arm flailing. He landed on his feet with a thud. Sharpened claws tore toward Gundack's stomach. He dodged sideways, half-stumbling on uneven ground.

His tail uncoiled, and he steadied. Tarr swung again, forcing Gundack to his left, a claw tip tearing skin below his open wound. Gundack's friendship hands clutched his bad arm. Sticky blood oozed between his fingers. Claws flashed toward his throat. Gundack jumped again. The tips of his claws raked Tarr's forearm and drew blood. Not enough.

His legs turned heavy, as though he trudged through deep sand. The image of the chalk returned, bathed in brilliant white light. What help was this? Gundack needed to reach different thoughts, clues to Tarr's battle strategy. How could a trader defeat such a warrior? Gundack evaded another swipe. He teetered and swung his tail in the opposite direction. How could he slash one of Tarr's main blood vessels and maintain balance at the same time? Oh, Talla, let him probe this raider's mind.

"You call yourself a ruler of the Red Desert?" Tarr's tongue dripped saliva. He spat on the ground. "An old kreness could fight better."

Such words had bite, but claws could kill. Tarr's insults were meant to distract him. Well, let that lackey of the God of Thieves try.

Tarr pressed forward, each rake of his hand coming closer. Images of darkness alternated with dazzling white light. Someone was falling. The bottom of Gundack's heels stung. His toes did, too. Sugarthorn. Tarr was pushing him toward the open edge of the plateau. Tarr must know about the bottomless holes. The raider had thought about Gundack's fall.

Tarr's claws grazed Gundack's shoulder. Gundack winced and jumped to the rear, landing ankle deep in sugarthorn. The surface felt different this time. The weight of his upper body seemed to pull him backward, as though his heels didn't rest on firm ground. Yet he couldn't have reached the brink of the plateau. Perhaps he stood on the edge of a hidden hole. Gundack slid one heel to the rear. Yes, a pit. Good. This one Gundack could use. He needed only to draw Tarr to the hole.

Gundack leaped backward and landed with a thud on solid ground. Tarr skirted around the hidden pit. The raider knew of this hole or guessed the trap awaited. Vermin. But other holes studded this area. The trick would be to find one that Tarr did not suspect. Then Gundack would have to distract the raider to make sure Tarr became the victim. Perhaps victory could be his.

Another swipe of Tarr's claws cut close to Gundack's side. He dodged to the right and panted. His heel found no ground upon landing. He swung his limbs and gained momentum to leap backward. Tarr advanced and faltered. No pit waited here, only a shallow depression. Tarr stumbled, and Gundack's claws grazed the raider's forearm. No visible damage and no show of pain in Tarr's expression. Gundack needed to inflict more damage than that.

Sugarthorn prickled Gundack's lower calf. The drop-off to Jular Plain wasn't far away. White light flashed again. Pale krenling fingers curled. The gods were offering these images from Tarr. Perhaps the krenling was a favorite slave. Certainly the chalk meant something important to Tarr.

Gundack slid one foot behind him. No firmness cradled his heel. This was another depression or a hole. Either way here was another opportunity for survival, perhaps his last. He had to enact his plan. He had to distract Tarr. Oh, Talla, cloud this raider's senses and deceive his yellow eyes.

"Such an ugly krenling of chalk awaits your return." Gundack braced every muscle he could. "Do you really think the linen robes

"He rasped and squealed, like a ledge lizard caught underfoot."

in my caravan—anything at all—could make that disgusting creature beautiful?"

Another roar filled the air. Tarr shook with fury. His eyes narrowed.

"I'll feed you to the lizard birds," Tarr shouted.

Tarr swiped at him with power. Gundack sprang away from the bloodied claws, leaping backward, beyond where the cavity must be. He arched his spine as his heels thudded against firm ground and let his legs slip out from under him. His rear landed in prickly sugarthorn. Gundack exhaled hard and half-closed his eyes. He must appear defeated. Would Tarr take the bait?

"Prepare to die," Tarr said.

He advanced toward Gundack, claw arm raised for a final strike. Contempt and rage filled his squinted eyes. Gundack's heart thundered. His temples throbbed. Whatever happened, he mustn't move until Tarr faltered or fell. Oh, Talla, let this be the final encounter between them. And let Eutoebi be his future.

Tarr lurched forward, yellow eyes wide. His legs plunged through a living mat of green sugarthorn. He sunk to his knees. This was a pit, not a mere depression. Horror swept across Tarr's face. His body shuddered and dropped further, his legs passing from view. He twisted and reached out with his two leathery battle arms, then reached above his head and thrashed air. He rasped and squealed, like a ledge lizard caught underfoot. Then his curved claws grasped around him at masses of spiny leaves, but they slipped through the vegetation, disappearing with the last view of his face, his expression, and his hate and anger.

The raider's howl swelled and faded, and Tarr was gone. Dead. Visions from the gods had brought victory. Gundack had avenged Talla. He was free to marry Eutoebi. Gundack scrambled to stand.

Blinding radiance pulsed in front of him. Pain tore though his body, as though his bones shattered.

If vengeance swallows the land, Tharda shall bring a white light to give strength to the least of us, and unbelievers will make heroes arise.

That hadn't been his thought. A force drew him downward. Ghostly crescent moons smiled from the morning sky. A krenling of chalk covered him with a blanket. Gundack's eyelids lowered. The krenling and the light were gone now. Tarr, too. Tarr was dead, wasn't he? His fall down the hole had been no vision. Gundack had maneuvered the mountain kren, the raider, the chosen one of the God of Thieves, to his death. He had succeeded in ending Tarr's life. Why then was he so tired? Strength to the least of us. Maybe if he slept for a while he'd feel stronger. And then too he'd understand what he'd done.

CHAPTER SEVEN

A DARK SECRET FESTERS

Grit coated Gundack's pasty tongue, as though he had licked sand. Something brushed against his battle arm. A sharp burning sensation shot from his shoulder to his wrist. He raised his eyelids. Daylight stung his pupils, even through protective membranes. He squinted, turned his head to the side, and groaned. Beyond his nose, a small black bug crawled across sandy soil. Gundack lay on his back on the ground.

Odors of lizard, kren and human blood blended with smoke and swirled into Gundack's nostrils. Had someone lit a funerary pyre? A sandship rasped out a vibrating moan. What if claws had gashed Zel? Gundack raised his head. Embers glowed in the fire circle, several kren-lengths away. A blackened cook pot sat clear of the coals. The contents of a trenching spade tumbled into the iron vessel. A tall kren with shiny hexagonal head scales and golden eyes held the tool's handle. Elar. Gundack detected the dank odor of pus worms, creatures used to heal wounds. Elar must be cleansing the worms with sand he had heated and cooled.

"Stay flat on your back," Rheemar's voice called.

Gundack blinked. The sun hung high as it slipped behind clouds, confirming the arrival of midday. Gundack had been unconscious for a while. And this fire had been built to treat gashes, not to cremate bodies. How many of Gundack's tribal kin had the raiders clawed?

"I haven't tied your compress in place." Rheemar approached, holding several rolled linen bandages. Claws had ripped the front of Rheemar's striped robe and tunic underneath. Irregular crimson blotches marred what remained. A wadded bandage covered the human's left shoulder. The raiders must have slashed the merchant man, before or despite the combat custom Gundack had invoked.

"Are you all right?" Gundack asked. "Are Sem and Zel and the others all right?"

"Mostly," Rheemar said. Dark lines shadowed his eyes. His shoulders sagged. The human was exhausted.

"Mostly can mean many things," Gundack said.

Rheemar knelt beside him, bending forward, his ebony braids dangling. He poked a meandering cluster of small, cream-colored worms under Gundack's bloodied dressing. The creatures writhed and squirmed. Worms wiggling within a wound always felt strange. Rheemar wrapped a strip of linen around Gundack's injured battle arm, then stood.

"They clawed everyone but Elar," Rheemar said. "Our gashes aren't as bad as yours." A sparkle filled the human's hazel eyes, then faded. Sweat glistened on his copper forehead and bearded chin. "I got your silver daggers back. Those mountain bastards retreated when they realized Tarr had fallen down that hole of no return."

Tarr. Yes. Tarr was gone, after ten long years. How had Gundack pushed the image of the raider's wide-eyed horror and desperate grasps to the back of his mind?

"We're all pretty lucky." Rheemar patted his own bandaged shoulder. "Time and a few shovelfuls of traitors will set things right."

Gundack grunted. Rheemar's news about injuries was welcome. How odd, though, for him to have used that particular expression about traitors. Eutoebi's father had often said the same thing. In ancient times, the gods' mutinous young lieutenants had imprisoned Father Sun. Then heroes had arisen and transformed the traitors into lowly worms. Ever since, the progeny of those foolish officers had purified the wounds of brave and honorable warriors in eternal demonstration of submission and remorse. Eutoebi rarely referred to pus worms as traitors. But her older brother, Kan, frequently had—at least, until he had become one himself.

A tiny cream-colored tail emerged from beneath Rheemar's bandage and oscillated. The human glanced down and shrugged. The thought of worms in a wound would have disgusted most humans. Rheemar not only understood the clawkren ways, he accepted them. Where had he gained his insight and wisdom?

"Your lips look dry," Rheemar said. "Would you like a drink of water?" He turned and retrieved a small water skin from behind a jagged rock.

"Just a little. Until I know I can keep more down."

Rheemar canted his oval head to one side. His pink tongue followed the track of his narrow lips. He turned his head from side-to-side, as humans sometimes did when perplexed. Then he pulled the stopper from the goatskin vessel.

"May water never turn to dunes," he murmured.

Northmen, even merchants, weren't known to initiate use of the Sandthardian water prayer, except by request. After all, humans had their own beliefs. Rheemar stared at Gundack. The skin on the man's forehead wrinkled. Yes, he waited for Gundack to finish the prayer, the way a tribal member would.

"And if water does turn to dunes," Gundack said, "may heroes arise to save desert tribes from doom." Gundack winked. "May they save worthy Northmen and their families, too."

"Did we become heroes today?" Rheemar squatted and placed the water skin in Gundack's friendship hands. He helped Gundack raise his head and shoulders. "I don't feel like a hero."

Gundack sipped the tepid water. Rheemar was familiar with desert beliefs. Obviously he did not understand them all.

"The prayer refers to the ancient heroes," Gundack said, "the ones who freed Father Sun and returned light to our world. There are no great heroes today. Just honorable krens and men who live ordinary lives."

Gundack took a little more water. He burped, then returned the water skin to Rheemar. The human's fist forced the stopper in place. He stood and leaned the crescent-shaped vessel against a rock. His eyes shut, as though he engaged in meditation. Something bothered the merchant.

"Let me read you." Gundack stretched his friendship arms toward Rheemar.

"This isn't a good time," Rheemar said.

"You have seen my weaknesses today," Gundack said, and patted the ground. "Why won't you let me see yours?"

Rheemar knelt. Gundack cradled the human's wrists in his palms. The human stiffened, then relaxed. His life pulse throbbed with a quick, steady rhythm. His skin felt cooler than it should. Rheemar feared something. Gundack could almost taste his discomfort.

"Do you worry," Gundack said, "that Tarr's younger brother, Yender, will be the next to bring trouble? Or that you won't find your sister now that Tarr is gone?"

"Both concern me," Rheemar said. "Must you do this?"

Rheemar jerked his wrists free and leaped to standing. He folded his arms against his chest. His upper front teeth pressed against his lower lip. Maybe the human's brain still harbored that loyalty pact idea.

"When two allies have bled side-by-side in a battle," Gundack said, "there is little need for their blood to intermingle." He raised himself to a sitting position. "Rheemar of the North, circumstances already bind us together. Yet there is something you fear to reveal."

Rheemar gazed skyward. Wind rippled the strips of his battle-torn robe.

"You plan a journey to the Mountain of the Dead," Rheemar said, "to seek Talla's blessing. Or so I have heard. I must discover if my sister's spirit now dwells there, too. Yet that mountain is particularly sacred to krens, living and dead. I dare not enter the Cave of Spirit Echoes without you."

Gundack grunted. Spirits disliked trespassers, especially human ones. Talla would protect Gundack. She had thought highly of Eutoebi's parents and would be pleased with his selection. But what deceased kren or kreness would shield Rheemar? Perhaps Gundack should place his hands on the human's shoulders, the way a sympathetic comrade might do. No, it probably was better to sit and listen. He clicked his tongue for Rheemar to continue.

"You and I will be traveling together," Rheemar said, "for at least one moon cycle. Eating together. Considering the thoughts written within each other's eyes."

"Most likely," Gundack said.

A dull ache washed through him, the pain from Rheemar's troubled mind. The human longed for solace. Did this conversation finally edge away from a dry well and toward a bountiful oasis?

"It is said." The merchant straightened the bandage on his sloped shoulder. His long fingers tucked a small cream-colored worm back in place. "That you can read the hearts of krens and men. That, given time, no secret can evade your power of perception." The human pulled himself to his full height, as though Gundack, sitting on the ground, towered above his slender frame. "Gundack of the Red Sands, I fear you above all else."

Gundack's ears flattened against his head. His wounded arm burned and throbbed. His tail coiled. This was not the dark secret festering inside his new ally.

CHAPTER EIGHT

A MOANING WIND

Gundack stood in a tangle of sugarthorn, tiny spines pricking his feet. He stared into the subterranean hole beyond his webbed toes. Blackness stared back. His friendship hand tossed in a small round stone. No soft thuds followed. This hole was deep. Tarr, or what remained of him, was down there somewhere. Only the gods knew how far. May Tarr's body imprison his wretched spirit for a thousand years.

Now what was that faint putrid odor? Rotting vegetation tucked inside unseen crevices? Or an infection in his wound? A sling bound his bandaged battle arm against his chest. The cloth and appendage smelled only of blood and worms. Gundack clutched his walking stick and crouched on one knee by the bore's edge. He sniffed, scrutinizing the air, the way Talla used to search their tent for hidden mildew. The scent was stronger now. Stinkwood. Mountain kren.

Tarr's body should have dropped to the ancient caverns, where the God of Thieves hid divine plunder. Perhaps this was not such a deep hole, after all. Of course, Tarr might have embedded his claws while trying to cling to the pit's upper wall. The force of his plunge could have separated claws from fingers. Or a sharp rock could have snagged part of his robe. No matter. A few small pieces of Tarr may linger nearby. The rest of him must be gone. Good riddance.

Oh, Talla. A thrust of claws could take so much away. Gundack rose and peered down from the plateau toward Jular Plain and the incinerated encampment. If only he could have Talla back. Ten years had not erased the memories of her soft spotted lips, cream-colored belly and firm brown and green thighs. Could he forget the way she would succumb to his embrace? Or her quiet strength when their only krenling—a son—had been born dead? Eutoebi, with her jewel-like head scales, was young, beautiful and his blood's desire. Love, like kettlefruit, took time to ripen. The gods had the power to give him that time.

Behind him, Sem clicked packing instructions to his caravan drivers. Two krens argued about the best way to load supplies onto Zel's back. Noises of life resounded. Yet on the plain below, strips of blackened hide flapped and fluttered against charred tent poles. The late afternoon wind hummed a plaintive tune. Banners of desolation reigned. So many merchants had died down there. How many of their families would be forced to sell all their precious heirlooms to survive the year? If they had not hunted Tarr, this might not have happened. Were he and Rheemar to blame?

Tarr and his raiders had deserved death. Tarr had deserved much worse. If only Gundack could have ripped out that vermin's entrails, then buried his screaming body in sand. Still, Gundack had avenged Talla without wanton blood lust—without staining his own personal honor. Yet ordinary revenge for murder, permitted by tribal laws, brought him little satisfaction. Tarr's spirit deserved to witness the torture and mutilation of his own family. But such thoughts could lead to dishonorable actions, deeds that would horrify Eutoebi. Gundack must control his anger and desires. Vengeance beyond careful customs would entitle others to vengeance of their own.

"We're nearly packed," Rheemar called to him. "Are you ready to proceed?"

"Not yet," Gundack said.

His caravan would descend from this plateau to the plain. There he and his comrades would search the rubble for tribal rings and amulets. Gundack and Sem were honor bound to return such possessions to grief-stricken mothers and widows. And, as a bearer of the bad news, Gundack would have to help the grieving mourn. Today he would face burned bodies, tomorrow charred lives.

Rheemar approached, leaning on his walking stick, his tight-lipped expression dour. A rusty clasp pin cinched his torn, blood-stained robe. Anger and weariness spilled from his hazel eyes. The aftermath of battle distressed him, as it should. Rheemar's real secret probably chewed at him, too.

"You don't have to do this, if you don't want," Gundack said. He gestured toward the remains of the merchants' encampment.

"How could I not do my part?" Rheemar inhaled and purged air through his nose, almost as flat as a kren's.

Gundack nodded. The human's words and musky scent hovered, so inescapable. Zel rasped a series of mournful sounds from the pack animal's circle. She, too, grieved. Zel would have known some of the sandship lizards who had perished in the conflagration. Wretched Tarr. Why had he pursued so much destruction?

Rheemar's long fingers adjusted the cloth sling cradling Gundack's arm, tucking in the flap at the elbow and smoothing the wrinkles. Pus worms wiggled beneath Gundack's bandage, producing a tingling sensation. It would be best to leave the creatures in place on his wound for several more days. But Elar should remove Rheemar's worms by tomorrow night. They would make the human sick if his wound sealed around them.

"Can you manage the path?" Rheemar said. "The bend below the sentinels is steep."

"I'll do well enough," Gundack said. "The path is the least of my problems."

Gundack tapped the foot of his walking stick on the ground. A nagging feeling returned. No merchant would have done such a thing. And no merchant had survived. But a driver kren might have been involved in the poisoning and fire. Particularly Rheemar's driver. That one might have found himself at Tarr's mercy. Such a disgusting creature. Such a traitor. Worse than Kan, and Kan had been bad enough. Kan had stolen Gundack's water amulet, decreasing the yields from tribal wells, producing too little water to wet down tents during the hottest days of the year. Elderly krens had died as a result. But this traitor had murdered an entire encampment. Old and young—even future krens would suffer from such an act. What shame that coward would bring upon his family, upon his whole tribe, should they discover his identity.

"Tarr should have been buried alive." Rheemar clenched his left hand into a tight fist. "In sand."

"The hole will have to do," Gundack said.

A lack of conviction in his own voice disturbed him. Shouldn't the deep bore be enough? After all, krens' dead bodies imprisoned their spirits until all flesh had decomposed or burned away. Corpses took years to rot in dry sand, yet Tarr's spirit would have more than enough time in that cavern to contemplate the consequences of his many evils.

"At least," Gundack said, "that son of a pus worm won't show up in the Cave of Spirit Echoes until long after we've left."

"His spirit isn't my greatest concern." Rheemar reached up and threaded his arm around Gundack's, the way a krenling might steady his aging grandfather. The human motioned toward the waiting caravan. "I wish I could be certain he's really gone. After we leave, his krens will return here to cremate their dead. Not all the Jular holes extend to the ancient caverns. Horizontal passageways link some below the surface. What if Tarr were still alive and they rescued him? What if he survives to strike back at those we love?"

Reports of Tarr's body rising from the dead had circulated on more than one occasion. Many mountain krens believed Tarr was an ancient hero reborn, and no mortal could ever slay him. In the natural world, all living beings could be killed. The gods would never change that. Gundack grunted. Plummeting into a deep hole should have broken Tarr's legs, hips and spine. Grasping for horizontal passageways would have ripped out claws and dislocated arms. Even if Tarr had survived, the wicked God of Thieves had only limited powers to heal his followers. Tarr would never engage in combat again. Such physical helplessness would be as bad as sitting in a rotting corpse. And raiders followed only the strong. They had little use for the injured and elderly.

"You fret too much," Gundack said to Rheemar, hoping he was right.

"Do I?"

Gundack glanced down at the top of the human's hairy head and felt the warmth of his arm. At least the merchant could admit his honest fears about Tarr. And how strong his grip was, despite his slight stature. Well, Gundack should expect no less from a human who could wield a hand sling with such power.

But Rheemar's inner strength needed nurturing. A secret weighed upon his soul. Probably something foolish, perhaps years ago. Gundack and his drivers shared their failings with each other. Later, Gundack would even admit his dishonorable thoughts about torturing Tarr's family. The best way to tame a dark, snarling desire was to flood the beast with light. But humans, even those who knew so many kren customs, resisted revealing their thoughts.

"Gundack," Rheemar said, "what am I going to do if I find my driver alive down there? If he was the one who started the fire for Tarr?"

Gundack stepped over a half-buried rock. The human and he had come to similar conclusions about the fire's origin. They thought alike in more than one way. But, if Rheemar had been close to his kren, that could prove troublesome.

"What would be done," Gundack said, "in the North where you come from?"

"We have a mayor in our village," Rheemar said, "and a judge." He stopped and faced Gundack, his chin tilted upward. "They would make the final decision."

A mayor and judge functioned something like tribal elders. They were good to have around. But krens on a trading journey had to settle matters. Swift justice was often necessary. Gundack tightened the sash around his waist and felt the weight of his silver dagger. At least desert krens had beliefs and customs to guide them toward fair and honorable outcomes.

"Is your driver a desert kren?" Gundack rested his friendship hands upon the human's shoulders.

"His mother was from the desert," Rheemar said.

"Then, if he started the fire," Gundack said, "he may choose to accept responsibility for his shame and cleanse the stain he has made upon his mother's honor." Gundack pressed his lips together. "Your driver might freely choose to meditate about his traitorous act. For a very long time."

Did the human understand what he meant? Gundack's claws tapped the spade end of his walking stick. The metal yielded a musical sound. Rheemar nodded, then stared straight ahead. Perhaps this human understood clawkren honor and therefore the justice of their customs.

ᔑ ᔑ ᔑ

How burnt everything smelled. Sometimes, the specific smell of charred tent hides surfaced in a breath of air. Incinerated human hair, kren flesh and lizard skin soon followed. Then remnants of entrails announced their grisly presence. Fire would have expanded and burst many internal organs. The myriad of odors huddled together, like travelers caught in a sandstorm, each one telling its own tragic tale.

"We should divide up," Gundack said.

"Look mainly for starstones, rings, bracelets and metal amulets." Sem's pointed ears angled one way and then another atop his head. He searched for sounds of danger or life, just as Gundack did.

"Elar," Gundack said, "come with me to where their sandships slept. The rest of you scour the remains of the tent camps. But watch out for smoldering embers." His tongue clicked instructions for Zel and the other lizards to keep watch for danger. Then Gundack lifted his trenching spade above his head. "Don't expect to find much else you can recognize."

"When you're done," Rheemar said, "may I see the jewelry?" He leaned on his walking stick and rubbed one sloped shoulder. "I knew most of . . ." His narrow lips pressed together. Dark half-circles lined the undersides of his eyes. "I would know where to bring many of the items we recover."

Rheemar stared toward the ground. How difficult for the merchant to lose a camp full of comrades and acquaintances. Gundack cupped his friendship hand around Rheemar's jaw. The human's face tilted upwards. Moisture gathered in those hazel eyes. What did humans feel when they cried? Probably as krens and sandship lizards did when they rasped out mourning wails, as though sand scratched a moaning wind.

CHAPTER NINE

MORNING PRAYER

Elar pressed his webbed foot against the flat upper edge of his trenching spade. He drove the pointed end into the ground. Then, with a guttural grunt, he raised the charred haunch of a sandship. Elar had not sustained injuries in the battle. He could do the heavy digging and lifting. Gundack would search for harness bells instead.

Gundack crouched. His claws sifted debris under the lizard's remains. This poor creature could have been Zel. Tension spread across Gundack's belly. Each clawkren tribe tooled metal in a distinctive and characteristic manner. What he found would be returned. Maybe even to families he knew. Recovery of belongings after a disaster was never an easy task.

Gundack's claws hit something firm. He brushed away charred particles and sand. Blackened sockets of a kren's skull stared upward, toward the late afternoon sun. Burnt flesh clung to the forehead, cheekbones and chin. This must have been one of the caravan drivers. Gundack's stomach felt heavy, full and queasy, as though it churned stones.

He turned his eyes away. A misshapen metallic lump lay nearby. Gundack held the small object in the palm of his friendship hand. Part silver? Probably melted. This had been some sort of amulet and might still contain power. Rheemar had hung an amulet at the entrance to his tent and had escaped death. He too believed in such things. Had his sister, Jardeen, worn one before Tarr had abducted her? Gundack added the object to his leather pouch.

The fire must have burned very hot to have melted metal. Gundack pinched a cooled cinder of facial flesh between his fingers and raised it to his nostrils. A hint of stinkwood resin. He sniffed other parts of the driver's blackened corpse. They too emitted that rancid smell. This kren had been coated with resin and then set afire, a common procedure at clawkren cremations to ensure rapid release of the spirit. But Tarr's krens would not have extended such a courtesy to one of their victims. Had this driver started the conflagration with lamp oil or fire resin, then immolated himself? His sandship lizard now covered him. Had his half-drugged lizard climbed on top of him and attempted to smother the flames before he, too, had succumbed? Such irony.

"Check over here," Elar said, still tipping the lizard haunch upward with his trenching spade. One of his friendship fingers pointed toward the ground. "There's something else. Under what's left of this creature's thigh."

Gundack saw a small pale green patch flecked with red-brown and amber. His claws pierced the blackened earth and discovered the hidden curve of an emerald bloodstone bracelet. Gundack freed the jewelry from its shallow grave and held the wrist band in the palm of his friendship hand. The diameter of this piece was too small to fit a kreness. Even Zydra, Eutoebi's best friend, a diminutive chalk, had thicker wrists. No, this bracelet had been created for a human girl—to be wedged over her right fist before puberty and, after her arm grew to adult size, never removed. Humans sometimes did that to protect their daughters from vengeful spirits.

Elar lowered the lizard haunch and motioned for Gundack to

move closer. His friendship finger rimmed a raised section of the bracelet, a delicate carved flower. The blossom had an odd shape, resembling two human hands pressed palm to palm.

"Looks like morning prayer," Elar said. "Remember that meadow full of pale purple flowers in the North last year?" He curled one claw hand into a fist and rubbed the tip of his flat nose with his knuckle. Then he reached up and scratched behind his pointed ears. "I didn't notice any human girls playing in the camp yesterday. Did you?"

"No, I didn't."

Gundack lowered his head and pressed the bracelet against his temples. No power emanated from the bloodstone. No breaks or cracks marred the bloodstone's polished surface. No signs that the jewelry had been forced off of an arm. Yet those tiny pits in the otherwise smooth surface suggested the bracelet might have been worn for several years. Or could fire have produced such marks?

"I'm sure this amulet was meant to be a gift for a man's daughter," Gundack said. "But it's either lost its force or not yet been consecrated."

"If we find any human." Elar curled his spotted tail, angled his spade underneath the sandship's lower chest and lifted. "Rheemar will probably want to bury his own kind, even if the body isn't ready."

Gundack clicked his tongue in agreement. His claws raked through ashes. Burying a human corpse showed respect, or so merchant men had told him. Interring a clawkren corpse, before reducing all flesh to cinders, would be an insult. Krens only treated traitors and murderers that way. Dishonorable spirits needed to cleanse their way of thinking before release.

"Looks like morning prayer."

Perhaps mankind's god of death freed all human spirits—even dishonorable ones—from their bodies as soon as breathing stopped. How foolish to unleash spirits of those who had harmed people and would do so again. No wonder human parents fitted young girls with permanent protective bracelets. Of course, humans and their deities had only recently traveled to Thard, little more than a thousand years ago. Maybe the human's god of death was a mere apprentice. Well, a few thousand more years of experience might improve his questionable reasoning skills.

"I'll gather all kren bones with flesh left on them," Gundack said to Elar. "You lay a ceremonial fire."

After all, who really knew if this driver had poisoned everyone's water and set the camp ablaze? Yet an ache radiated from somewhere deep inside Gundack. Someone besides the murdered merchants deserved to suffer. Gundack stretched and brushed ashes from his robe. He must control his gnawing suspicions and desires. Without definite proof, Gundack had no right to insult the immolated kren's family, tribe or remains.

The afternoon sun was lowering. Already a small campfire burned upon the top of Jular Steeps. Tarr's raiders, or what remained of them, had not fled far. The time neared for Gundack and his krens to share the evening meal, assign watch duties and set up the sleeping circle. Yet something about the carved flower tickled a distant memory.

Pale purple flowers. In the North, Gundack had once met a dark-skinned merchant man with coarse ebony locks and a persistent cough. His plump hazel-eyed wife had planted flower beds around their cottage and grown lavender-colored blooms. Morning prayer. She had engraved an unusual human word for garden into a brass plate on her wooden fence—jardin.

A cold feeling with the force of a winter gale swept through Gundack. This bracelet had never been cut away from an arm. But might an arm have been cut off to release the bracelet? He clutched the circle of bloodstone in a death grip, ears flat against his head. Jardin. Jardeen. Rheemar's abducted sister.

CHAPTER TEN

PART KREN

Father Sun spread his pink and lavender robe wide, preparing to
slip behind the Divider Mountains. Gundack stood on the plain
and surveyed the plateau where Tarr had died that morning. Wind
tumbled balls of dry brush near the vermin's grave. No evidence of
living raiders up there. But high above that barren table, atop Jular
Steeps, twin campfires now flickered. Only one fire had burned a
while ago.

Evening wind carried the smell of death. Gundack detected
something more, though. He sniffed several times. His tongue
tasted the air. A faint bitterness. Yes, he smelled the resin of
stinkwood. The raiders prepared pots of the sticky substance to
cremate their dead. That driver's immolated corpse had smelled
of stinkwood resin. Gundack could almost see the kren's charred
skull—those two hollow eye sockets.

Gundack maneuvered his bulky pack near the campfire. He
tightened his belly muscles and tried not to stare at his caravan
drivers, who had gathered around the fire. Most of them sat on
the ground and sorted through recovered bells and amulets. A few
worked beside Rheemar, preparing dinner. The gleam of life in
their yellow eyes was so beautiful. Life. The gift of life. Now he
could look forward to his Eutoebi.

"Do you recognize these markings?" A driver handed a small

harness bell to his best friend. "I've never seen so many flamboyant swirls in brass."

"My wife's second cousin married into a family who over-decorates everything." The kren lifted the bell toward his eyes, tilted his head to one side and frowned. "I'll have to view this in the morning to be sure."

"Let me have a look," Gundack said.

Gundack studied the brass bell but couldn't identify who had done the casting. Just as well. He returned the bell, then fingered the soft texture of the worn leather pouch around his waist and the firmness of the concealed bloodstone bracelet. So far, only Elar knew of the bracelet's discovery. What if Gundack was right about Jardeen? Why would Tarr steal her only to mutilate her? The bag tugged at his waist-sash, as though made of iron. A bracelet shouldn't feel this heavy. Perhaps the carved morning prayer retained some power, after all.

He glanced toward Rheemar. The human squatted on the other side of the fire circle, his thick black braids forward of his shoulders. Slender bronze fingers arranged kettlefruit and shelled nuts on a small platter. His nose scrunched. He barely breathed. After digging a mass grave, Rheemar appeared in no mood to eat.

The pungent, oily odor of nutmeats clung like dried blood to the lining of Gundack's nose. He, too, had no appetite. Yet to survive—to marry Eutoebi and have krenlings—he must eat. A burning sensation spread across his chest. He burped. This afternoon's dig had been hard on both stomach and mind.

Rheemar. The human's torn, bloody robe was a mess, and he had lost his possessions in the fire. Ten days ago, Gundack had traded a silver clasp pin for a juvenile krenling's linen tunic, robe and belly-wrap. Perhaps the clothing would fit Rheemar. Gundack unstrapped his pack and burrowed beneath his own spare robe. Yes, an older krenling's garments might do. He called Rheemar's name.

"Do you need something?" The human rose.

"No," Gundack said, "but you do. Come."

Rheemar ambled around the drivers and toward Gundack.

"Tomorrow morning," Gundack said, "after we're done digging, we should all change our clothes." He stood and offered the gift to the human. "You don't have to wear the belly-wrap. After all, humans never crawl on your stomachs down mountains."

"They're beautiful." Rheemar fingered the woven yellow fabric. Uncertainty filled his eyes. "I—I couldn't."

"We are allies." Gundack rested his claw hand upon Rheemar's shoulder. "Think about it."

The human nodded and stepped back, as though to turn. He lowered his head and spread one hand against his face.

"Your offer means much to me," Rheemar said. "My blood is part kren."

Part kren? How could a clawkren and human produce a child? Gundack must have misunderstood. But, wait. Hadn't Rheemar requested a blood alliance the night before? Hadn't the human projected only transient fear of a pact's potential consequences? Gundack had assumed Rheemar didn't understand the danger or showed poor judgment. But had he already sealed and survived such a pact?

"You need to explain," Gundack said.

"Years ago." Rheemar crossed his arms against his chest and rubbed them, as though he were cold. "A desert kren, one of your tribe, and I found ourselves in a dangerous situation. We were total strangers, yet had to trust each other as brothers to escape death. We cut our arms and bound them together for a full turn of the sandglass. After our pact was complete, we planned our strategy. We got bad chills and fever before the next moon cycle. But, by then, we had evaded those who had intended to kill us and sealed our fates by blood."

Might this human's heart truly pump the blood of Gundack's tribe? It would be good to read him again, but not against his will. Gundack extended his friendship hands toward Rheemar, palms turned upward. But the human tucked his arms behind his own back.

"A desert kren," Gundack said, "would let a brother read him."

"This human cannot." Rheemar turned and ambled back to the campfire.

Gundack closed his pack. The gods must have approved of the man's alliance. Otherwise, he would not have survived. Might they also want Rheemar to know about the bloodstone bracelet and the kren's skull? If so, how and when should Gundack tell him?

🌀　🌀　🌀

Gundack stepped over to the campfire and warmed his hands. Sem dropped fresh sugarthorn leaves into a blackened kettle of boiling herbal broth. Mountain sugarthorn had little character and, unlike the northland variety used for tea, tasted best when boiled with other plants. The churning brew spit liquid onto hot stones. The lead driver's tail protruded from beneath his robe and curled. He rubbed the oval marking on his cheek, as though the scarlet pigmentation made his skin itch. Sem always touched that blotch when he worried.

"We're going to need more food and water." Sem's finger tapped his chin, the rhythm irregular. Then he wiggled each one of his ten friendship fingers and two friendship thumbs in succession. He was counting. "Before we journey to the Mountain of the Dead." His hexagonal crimson and green head scales, usually glistening, dulled in the fading twilight. "No offense intended, Rheemar, but I didn't pack for a man."

"You worry too much." Elar placed a mound of nutmeats on the kettlefruit platter and winced. "Another day of dealing with body parts, and none of us will want to eat for a month."

"I'd grow sun catchers," Rheemar said, "like yours if I could, and nourish myself." He draped two crescent-shaped sections of dried kettlefruit on top of his head. A tentative grin protruded through his whiskers. His gaze met Gundack's. "Would I fit in better with head scales?"

"I've never met any human," Sem said, "who couldn't out-eat a sandship lizard. That is, when he felt well." The kren tossed another handful of sugarthorn into the pot. "As for fitting in, we all do that best when we accept ourselves."

"Then, I'm afraid," Rheemar said, "I'll have to accept who I am." He shrugged and peeled the dark brown kettlefruit slices off his head, returned them to the platter and extracted a clinging strand of black hair from the food. "We'll need to travel to Jular Village for provisions. The town's four or five days away, but fairly safe. Well, usually."

Gundack nodded and sat on the ground. The group was making light of a miserable day and a potentially serious situation. Rheemar was trying to make up for withholding his earlier thoughts.

A round trip to the village for food and water would be essential, although it would delay their journey to the Mountain of the Dead. How many full water skins would they deplete as they hiked to that mountain? How many days would they spend searching for water after they arrived? Numbers swirled through Gundack's mind, like leaves tumbling in boiling broth. As long as all else went well, he could still make it back to his tribal encampment by the day of marriages.

"We need to finish digging," Gundack said, "and be packed to travel by tomorrow afternoon." He gestured toward the campfires up on the Steeps. "I think those sons of pus worms will have too much spare time in another day or so. I don't want to stay here any longer than necessary."

Sem and the other krens grunted in agreement. Rheemar kept rearranging the kettlefruit slices and nutmeats on the platter, his lips pinched tight, as though he played some sort of strange game. Finally, he stood and stretched. His fingers fidgeted with the soiled bandage on his shoulder. Then he stepped back from the fire circle, turned toward the plateau and Steeps, and scratched his beard. If men had tails, Rheemar's would have twitched.

Gundack cupped his claw hand over his leather pouch. There would never be a good time to initiate conversation about the bloodstone bracelet. Yet this moment might be better than most. Should he talk to the human in private? But, when Gundack delivered the news about Jardeen's disfigurement and probable death, kren customs would require him to help Rheemar mourn. A fellow clawkren would never ask for more than a day. Yet Rheemar, a human, might. What if he asked to travel with Gundack for three moon cycles, the maximum period of obligation? Gundack would have little time to spend alone with Eutoebi, even on the day of marriages.

Still, Rheemar had survived a blood pact with a desert kren. He deserved treatment as a tribal member. Gundack would lose honor if he didn't disclose knowledge about Jardeen. He clicked his tongue to get the human's attention.

"Elar and I were discussing flowers," Gundack said, "while we were digging." He made a discreet motion toward Elar to remain quiet. "I seem to recall a merchant in the north who liked flowers. His wife grew a lot of morning prayer."

"Oh?" Rheemar pivoted and faced Gundack. He canted his head, his hazel eyes narrow and brimming with uncertainty.

"Merchants tend to congregate in similar places." Gundack stood and straightened the sling on his wounded arm. "Did you ever meet that man?"

"My parents," Rheemar said, "kept a garden full of morning prayer."

Queasiness spread through Gundack's empty stomach. Rheemar had dragged each word out, as though he feared to complete the sentence. Gundack had hoped his theory about the bracelet would prove incorrect.

"Come over here," Gundack said. He patted his leather pouch. "Elar and I found something under a sandship lizard near your tent. There was a body, a kren, there, too. "

Gundack's friendship fingers dipped into the hide pouch, the action cloaked by his claw hand. The human waited, eyes blinking, the rise and fall of his chest even. Gundack wiggled the bloodstone bracelet free from the bag.

"I think your driver might have had this," Gundack said, "when he set himself afire."

He offered the bracelet. Amber flecks in the stone glistened in the moonlight. An expression of pain and terror flashed across Rheemar's face, with the speed of an enemy's strike.

"No," Rheemar whispered.

The human clamped his jaws together. His body stiffened. He tore the bracelet from Gundack's grasp and clutched it against his chest. Gundack reached for Rheemar. The human, crying, raised one arm across his face and twisted to escape. Gundack grasped him with all four hands, careful not to dig claws into flesh. He pulled the human against him, feeling the throb of his chest, the hot face pressed against his belly. A long wail erupted. The mountains echoed his agony.

"Don't fear me, brother," Gundack said, "or my gift of perception."

Gundack shifted his hands, one by one, until his arms encircled his ally and held him fast. Rheemar no longer struggled.

"I want to kill Tarr ten thousand times." The human's chest heaved against Gundack's thighs. Human sweat grew pungent, even stifling. His small, miserable body shuddered.

"Oh, Gundack," he whispered, his voice hoarse, "such dishonorable thoughts fill me and corrupt my very heart."

Gundack stroked the back of the human's head, feeling the coarse texture of his hair and reading the inner chaos he projected. He could almost see the tiny triangular head scales of a very young mountain krenling—a small bludgeoned face smeared with bright chestnut blood. Perhaps a son or nephew of Tarr. Rheemar's ugly desires were not so different from the ones Gundack had fought earlier today.

"We wage our deadliest battles," Gundack said, "against ourselves."

"But what if I lose?" Rheemar said. "If my actions dishonor desert krens and water becomes sand?"

Dishonor krens? Turn water to sand? In the ancient days, the gods had made a promise to Gundack's ancestors. Their tribe would rule the Red Sands until water turned to dunes. No human transgression could cause such a calamity, only a great loss of tribal honor. Yet Rheemar's blood was both human and clawkren. Might his deeds provoke the gods in such a manner? Gundack pulled away from him. His claw hands cradled the human's bearded face. Grit flecked those soft whiskers. Rheemar's skin was so hot.

"Vow you'll stop me," Rheemar said, "if I ever unleash my fury upon—upon someone helpless or innocent."

"If I am there," Gundack said, "I'll do all I can."

Gundack reached for the human's hands but they closed into fists. Ties between them grew stronger as though the smaller were son to the kren. But trust was slow to flower. Would it ever fully bloom?

"I don't know if all of Jardeen is dead," Gundack said, "or just one hand."

"Yet I must mourn." Rheemar stared up into Gundack's eyes. "May I still travel with you to the Mountain of the Dead? I don't want to be alone."

"I understand your loneliness, your dark thoughts," Gundack said. "You may travel with us, but wear the robe and tunic I offered you."

He grunted and studied the silvery flecks in Rheemar's pupils. Tension coiled Gundack's tail. His own lust for blood revenge had not been satisfied by Tarr's death. Gundack turned toward Jular Steeps and let the wind hit his face. Would such rage ever cool?

THE
CAVE
OF
SPIRIT ECHOES

CHAPTER ELEVEN

WRINKLED KETTLEFRUIT

Aromas of incense and fragrant leaves wafted from one merchant's table. Gundack pushed through the crowded marketplace, Sem and Rheemar on his right. The sharp odor of urine-tanned goat hides drifted from a stall. Pungent cheeses and dried kettlefruit. Bridal tea bowls and krenling toys. Poisons, spears and crematory resins. Jular Village sold items for all occasions.

"I'll need a climber's pack," Rheemar said, his voice competing with hawking vendors, rattling wares and the throng's rasps and chatter. "I'll also need a sturdy rope."

A kren in a yellow and brown striped robe jostled Rheemar and kept going. Gundack flinched. That kren had notched ears and triangular head scales, as Tarr's raiders had. Yet Gundack detected no smell of apprehension from Rheemar. The human had ignored the mountain kren. How strange, after all that had happened on Jular Plateau.

"We've got plenty of pack rope with the caravan." Sem tightened the sash on his robe and glanced behind him. His friendship hand clasped the hilt of his silver dagger. "Ought to work well enough to move packs between rock overhangs."

"You don't understand," Rheemar said, slowing his pace. "I'll need a climbing rope. For a grapnel."

"A grapnel?" Gundack laughed. What was this human thinking? He skirted around a band of human children, dressed in rags and pushing each other. He patted the money pouch hidden under his robe. Still safe. "We're not planning to scale walls and raid a village. Or cliffs to battle Tarr's krens. We're going to climb the Mountain of the Dead."

"Not without a good rope." Rheemar's thick, black eyebrows knitted together. "I'm sure you've heard of sucker slimes."

Sucker slimes. Those tiny, bright-orange creatures liked to burrow under head scales, claws and nails. They drew moisture from their victims and could turn hands and feet into black, mucous-covered stumps. A case of the slimes wasn't as deadly as molders—another flesh-eating disease—unless head scales became infected. And slimes, unlike molders, didn't force victims to conceal disfigured faces under hoods for the rest of their lives. Still, slimes caused a bad disease. A good thing they couldn't survive in sand. In fact, Gundack only had encountered their colonies around docks in the port cities of Nath and Blane.

"Slimes need water," Sem said. "The Mountain of the Dead is a desert in the sky. Anyone who told you slimes are up there has them growing in their brains."

Rheemar pointed toward the far end of the marketplace. Gundack let his gaze follow. Multicolored rugs hung from poles, as though they were bride's banners. On the day of marriages, what color would Eutoebi's banner be? Coils of rope were stacked on an adjacent table. Rheemar darted off in that direction, again colliding with the kren in the yellow and brown striped robe. Tarr's raiders had worn such robes. Gundack scratched his shoulder. Mountain krens often had little use for humans. And, in this crowd, anyone could shove a knife into a belly and escape free and clear. Was this one here to harm Rheemar? Gundack was honor-bound to watch

"Eutoebi always dried and cured kettlefruit the same way."

over Rheemar while they journeyed together. Nothing to do but follow the human and keep him out of trouble.

"We're looking for a sturdy rope," Rheemar said to the merchant kren sitting beside the table. The human raised his left hand, fingertips together, the signal that he understood Kren. Then he motioned for Gundack and Sem to move closer. "For traveling the mountains."

"Ah," the rope merchant said with a rasp.

The kren, a little shorter than Sem, wore an indigo robe over a matching tunic. His blotchy friendship hands rested against his portly belly. He had the triangular head scales of a mountain kren, but with bright scarlet and green pigmentation. His breath smelled of spiced nutmeats and liquor. This merchant probably lived in the Northland and had the habit of overindulgence.

"I've got exactly what you need." The merchant kren yanked a coil of rope out of his stack and slapped the bundle on the wooden table. "It's only been used a few times. I'll give you a good price."

Rheemar ran his fingers over the coil and tilted his head to one side. He rubbed his chin whiskers. His pink tongue moistened his lower lip.

"Will this support the weight of a desert kren?" Rheemar said.

The merchant's eyes scrunched down to slits. His two brown and green ears, tips folded down, pointed in the human's direction. Krens used their claws when climbing. Ropes were for emergencies or handling packs. Raiders, on the other hand, used ropes to attack from cliff-tops or to scale city walls. Gundack didn't need much perception to know what bothered the kren.

"You think I sell to thieves?" the rope merchant said.

"No." Rheemar set both hands on the table and grinned. "I'm

a merchant. My comrades are traders. We're used to being called thieves and take no offense at your remark. Sometimes we travel the Divider Mountains. Sometimes we don't. But there are places where we need to avoid touching sucker slimes. Climbing straight up a rope is the best way."

"Sucker slimes, eh?" The merchant clasped his friendship hands together and rotated the leathery thumbs around each other. He stared at Gundack, then back at Rheemar. "You trade flesh on the docks of Nath and Blane?"

"No," Rheemar said, resting his knuckles against one hip. "We have honor."

Something to Gundack's right moved. The notch-eared kren appeared in his peripheral vision. Green blotches covered his forehead and one arm bore the jagged mark of a healing wound. Had he fought in the battle on Jular Plateau? A pot of trouble might be ready to boil over the rim. Time to buy food and get going.

Gundack tightened his robe sash and stepped forward. He was a head taller than the rope merchant and more muscular. He rested his claw hand on Rheemar's shoulder.

"My friend has a few strange ideas about climbing," Gundack said. "What do you expect? He's only a man." Gundack fingered the line's rough texture. This rope had decent quality, better than most. "Two starstones."

"Four," the merchant said.

"Three," Gundack said, his voice firm. "No more."

Rope and money changed hands. Sem slung the coil around his shoulder. Gundack tied his pouch back in place and let his gaze sweep over the nearby crowd. Where had that mountain kren gone?

"Well done," Rheemar said. "I'll meet you back where the food and water stalls are. I'm going to an amulet shop up the next street to replace mine lost in the fire. The one against poison insects that used to dangle at the entrance to my tent. And I still need a pack."

"We should go with you," Gundack said. The same notch-eared kren stepped from behind a stall stacked with spears. He pressed his way around nearby shoppers, cut between Sem and Rheemar, then moved toward an incense display. "Something around here feels wrong."

"I'll be fine," Rheemar said.

"Then don't take long," Gundack said.

Rheemar turned, faced the spear stall and disappeared into the crowd. Gundack signaled for Sem to follow the human. That notch-eared kren had questionable intentions. Hadn't Rheemar noticed his recurring presence?

Gundack took long strides to the kettlefruit displays. The wrinkled pieces, adorned with a moderate selection of bugs, would have the most flavor and character. Eutoebi always dried and cured kettlefruit the same way. She would be a good wife. Gaining Eutoebi would be worth the journey to the Mountain of the Dead.

"I passed by the amulet shop," Sem said, nudging Gundack's side. "Our little friend was inside." The driver sounded as though he had bit into a twig of rancid-tasting stinkwood. "I hid in the passageway between buildings and waited. Two mountain krens left the shop and headed for an alley. One was that notch-eared son of a pus worm from before. Rheemar walked out the same door shortly thereafter. He watched them, one hand cupped over his mouth, until they disappeared into the shadows. Then he hurried in the opposite direction. Rheemar should be back here soon. Or not at all. The krens wore emerald bloodstone bands."

Emerald bloodstone bands. Tarr's krens or members of his family. Gundack stuffed the kettlefruit purchase into his backpack. Had those lackeys of the God of Thieves threatened Rheemar? Or purchased his loyalty? Would the alliance building between Gundack and the human crumble to dust?

CHAPTER TWELVE

INNER PRESSURE

The Mountain of the Dead loomed in the distance, at least a day's journey away from the foothill where Gundack stood. Pink and gray clouds draped the volcano's jagged black silhouette. Gundack was nearer the mountain than he had ever been. He glanced toward Rheemar, then at his caravan drivers. They stood motionless and straight, facing the volcano, bodies as tense as taut lines. Even Zel and the other lizards were rigid and quiet. A pressure welled within Gundack, as though he were a sealed pot of boiling broth hung over a fire. Perhaps no living creature could visit this place and feel at ease.

"Our father used to tell me," Sem said to Elar, "nobody alive enters the Cave of Spirit Echoes and leaves in that same favorable condition." He unplugged a small water skin and took a hearty swallow, as though the drink might be his last. "Our mother claimed escape was possible only if the spirit of a hero intervened."

"Every time she'd tell me that," Elar said, "I'd get this preposterous idea." He motioned for the water skin. "Remember our third cousin, the one who kept repeating himself? He must have had ten thousand pointless stories. I used to think I'd take him into the cave with me and get him talking. I figured, after listening to him, the ancient heroes would let us live forever."

"I'll enter the cave alone," Gundack said. "My need to fulfill my vow to Talla and ask her blessing must not endanger any of you."

An anxious look spread across Rheemar's bearded face. The skin on his forehead furrowed and pushed at his eyebrows. The ominous mountain had not dissuaded him from seeking Jardeen's spirit. He was determined.

"I must go with you," Rheemar said. The tufts of his black braids looked like two frayed ends of rope. "To mourn for Jardeen or the part of her Tarr hacked away."

"And you'll need my help," Sem added, rubbing the red blotch on the side of his cheek. "Sometimes I forget how many years I've been your lead caravan driver. No matter how hard I've tried, I've never forgotten all the pointless tales you and your tribal kin have ever told me."

Sem extended his friendship hands for Gundack to read him. The kren's life pulse throbbed hard, from a mixture of fear and love. Gundack could almost touch Sem's thoughts. If only Rheemar could be as open as Sem. Had anything transpired between Rheemar and the two mountain krens in the amulet shop? Should he confront the human? No, Gundack had brought Rheemar the news about Jardeen and must offer company and comfort. For now.

"Then," Gundack said, "it must be the three of us."

His eyes fixed on the massive depression in the mountaintop. The sun lowered behind the caldera, as though being swallowed. Ancestor krens had believed that Father Sun slept there among the spirits each night. No wonder. The dry, barren volcano had not erupted since the ancient days. The home of the spirits stayed as dead as its occupants. Dead. He pictured Talla in her scarlet robe, pointed ears tipped forward, telling bedtime stories to their tribe's many krenlings. So long ago.

"During the time of creation," Talla had said, "the wind imprisoned Tharda below the rocky plains. To escape, Tharda ripped through the world's crust, thrusting up giant stone slabs to form the mountains."

How elegant Talla's high cheek bones and rounded chin had been. And when she had described Father Sun carrying Tharda to the largest star in the sky, not one krenling had even whispered. Gundack could still hear her eerie moans, see her jaws snap as she depicted the enraged wind biting off the sun's tail. That plunging, fiery tail had transformed the Mountain of the Dead into a volcano. Oh, Talla. Her stories never had been pointless. Only her death.

Gundack clicked orders to his drivers to unload the lizards' packs and set up camp. The area was flat enough, at least in places, to accommodate the traditional tea ceremony and sleeping circle. They would all benefit from tea and a good night's rest. He moved over to Zel and helped Elar unstrap several hide-covered packs. The feeling of inner pressure lingered in his head and gut.

"Sem and I must prepare our minds to face tomorrow," Gundack said to Elar. "You will be in charge until we return. Would you and one of your brothers-in-law share night watch?"

Elar rested his claw hand atop Gundack's and nodded. His eye membranes slid open, yellow pupils staring into the distance.

"How many days," Elar said, "do you think you'll be up there?"

Gundack grunted. Travel to and up the mountain would take at least three days. Gods willing, they'd avoid serious injuries and the return trip would remain uneventful. How much time would he need in the Cave of Spirit Echoes? Gundack concentrated on Tharda's star, then bowed his head. If the mother of worlds knew the answers to his questions, she kept them to herself.

"Let me put my question another way," Elar said. "How many days do you want us to wait before we search for you?"

"You're not to search for us," Gundack said. How disquieting his own words were. "Wait until Brother Moon's next cycle. Then return to the Red Sands."

"We can't leave you." Elar stepped back.

Gundack hoisted a sealed pack of fine linens off Zel's back and lowered it to the dusty ground. For ten years, he had vowed to slay Tarr and carry the story of his victory to Talla. Yet Gundack's wits, not his claws, had taken that notch-eared vermin's life. He must fulfill this final duty to his wife.

Talla. How he loved her. If he died in the cave, would it really be so terrible? Surely she would visit him every day until his body decayed. Then, when his spirit was finally free, they would dwell together forever. No, Gundack was too young to resign himself to death. His desire for Eutoebi had not waned. He unloaded a rolled carpet. The rug landed on the dirt with a thud. He had a duty to carry on his family line. Besides, members of their tribe needed the goods and starstones Gundack's sandship lizards carried. Otherwise, they would be no better off than the families of those murdered merchants on Jular Plain. He had pursued Tarr for this fulfillment.

"If we don't return on our own," Gundack said to Elar, "we will have already left you."

CHAPTER THIRTEEN

A DAMAGED SECTION OF LINE

Gundack raised his tail, sat on a flat boulder and rubbed his neck. He, Sem and Rheemar would begin their climb up the mountain soon. Midday sunlight warmed Gundack's back. This should have been a comfortable place to rest. Yet something irritated him, as though sucker slimes burrowed under his scales. As though an enemy tracked him. He turned his head and glanced at Rheemar.

"I thought you'd never decide to stop." Rheemar sat down and pressed against his back, well below the shoulder blades. The human had been complaining about lava bits in his sandals. Snapping about everything. Did Rheemar experience the same uncomfortable feelings as Gundack? Or had he treacherous thoughts that brought guilt?

Gundack unwrapped the hide strips from his feet, his claws snagging the bindings. Several small, sharp pieces of crumbled lava had embedded themselves in the coverings. No cuts showed on his heels or in the webbing between his toes. The balls of his feet were tender, though. He bent one knee and crossed his leg over his thigh. What a pleasure to massage a foot. Gundack plucked lava bits out of the hide wrappings. How fortunate he had been born a desert kren. He would never again complain about trudging over dunes.

"Why do you do this?" Rheemar said to Gundack. He motioned for Sem to come over and rest, too. "How will you even know if Talla gives you her permission to remarry?"

"I'll leave the cave alive," Gundack said. He made room on the rock for Sem. Survival would be the best acknowledgement of Talla's blessing he could hope to receive.

"And how will I know," Rheemar said, "whether or not Jardeen is finally free from torture? Whether some mountain bastard isn't slowly hacking her to bits?"

"You'll know something for sure," Sem said, "if you don't leave the cave alive." Sem shrugged his shoulders, then put one foot against the boulder, bent over and massaged his knee. "This is a miserable place. All those who Tarr has murdered are unloading their wrath and frustration upon us."

Gundack nodded. Sem was right. He wiggled his toes, then scraped gravel from underneath a curved claw. He had never liked wrapping his feet in hides. How did mountain krens deal with sharp rocks all the time? Perhaps sore feet contributed to an irritable disposition. No wonder Tarr had brought so much misery.

Gundack stretched his claw arms. Other widower krens took new brides without journeying to the Mountain of the Dead. Yet Talla had been so special. She had always been sensible, hopeful. And forgiving. Her presence in the cave might dissipate his dishonorable lust for blood revenge. He wanted to live the rest of his life in peace, with Eutoebi, with krenlings of their own. Someday, he, Talla and Eutoebi would dwell together in the Cave of Spirit Echoes. Talla's blessing now would ensure eternal harmony later. Was that too much to ask now that Tarr must be dead?

"Do you see that bulge?" Sem stood straight as a tent pole and looked upward, one claw hand shading his eyes. "Almost halfway to the caldera."

Gundack squinted. What did Sem see? Oh, yes, there it was. An unusual curved rock formation with rust-colored streaks tilted against the jagged black mountainside. The smooth, rounded stone must be two kren-heights or so in diameter. How odd he hadn't noticed it earlier.

"The cave is guarded by Tharda's tipped tea bowl," Sem said. "That's what my mother used to say. She told me never to climb the mountain without an offering of tea." He patted the bulge of the leaf pouch he always carried under his robe. "I never thought I'd travel here alive."

"My father told me not to worry about the tea." Gundack studied the rock formation, their probable climbing destination. "He said to follow the spirits' breath once inside the cave."

"If sucker slimes get us first," Rheemar said, "all that advice won't matter. This will be a good place to inspect our ropes."

Why did Rheemar insist that sucker slimes thrived on the mountain? Well, it wouldn't hurt to humor him. Gundack walked over the uneven ground to the packs.

"I want to check the one I'll use," Rheemar said.

Gundack pulled out two coiled ropes and brought the newer one to the human. This was a hefty line, worth the price he had paid at Jular Village. Then Gundack stood near his own pack, legs apart, and hung the older coil on one battle arm. He unrolled his line, segment by segment, and, with the help of both friendship hands, rewound and hung the rope around his opposite battle arm. He focused upon each section. Was it frayed? Would it give too much when taut? And, if he had to knot this rope together with Rheemar's, would the union hold under stress? Now there was an interesting question, both practical and metaphoric.

His gaze returned to Tharda's Bowl. Was that a narrow ledge leading to the formation? Yes, it connected with an irregular path that curved along much of the mountainside.

"Maybe," Gundack said, "we won't need ropes. My ancestors used their claws to climb. I wouldn't want to offend them."

"Then pray you sprout wings." Rheemar pointed toward the right, his pink lips spread in a thin smile. "Do you see that series of ledges cut into vertical rock? A walkable path doesn't start until you reach the top overhang, because of crusted sucker slimes. They grow in the crevices of the black rock, too."

"What makes you think so?" Sem said. He knotted the binding around his foot covering. "Have you been here before?"

"There's something I never told you." Rheemar tightened his grasp around his rope. "At first, I didn't trust you. Then, after Tarr fell down that hole, I thought it didn't matter anymore. But it matters now."

"So you have traveled here," Gundack said.

"Yes," Rheemar said. "Not all the way to the cave, but close. And Tharda's Bowl marks more than the Cave of Spirit Echoes. It's Tarr's winter hiding place. That's why no one ever found him."

Tarr had wintered in the Mountain of the Dead? Impossible. Well, maybe once. Even twice. But year after year? There were more than enough spirits of his victims up there to have eliminated him. How had he managed to protect himself? Had he draped himself in amulets?

And how had Rheemar—a human—journeyed this way before and survived? This was mountain kren territory, ruled by the tribe of the emerald bloodstone rings. Men had pushed that tribe out of the northern meadowlands seven hundred years ago. Not by force, but by clever use of clawkren tribal laws. Mountain krens had resented humans ever since and supported aggressive leaders such as Tarr. Even those krens who still farmed the northland looked the other way when Tarr's raiders attacked people's villages. No human—let alone one on his own—was welcome beyond Jular Steeps.

"Tarr's cave, eh?" Gundack inspected another section of rope. The fibers emitted a faint odor of rot and felt rougher than they should. "Your ideas about Tarr and sucker slimes are very imaginative. Have you been using mottleflower?"

"Two mountain krens my own age," Rheemar said, "traveled here with me. They taught me and made sure I didn't touch the slimes. At first, I didn't trust them. Didn't even want to be with them. Yet I didn't feel safe alone. One night, they put a sleeping potion in my water skin. I didn't notice it, but I knew the next morning. It felt as though my head would explode. I can still see those two krens laughing. Their triangular head scales practically vibrated."

Gundack stared hard at Rheemar. How careless the human had been. Like Kan. Youth and folly had led one astray and granted wisdom to the other.

"They promised not to kill me," Rheemar said, "at least not on purpose. Said they liked having me around. My stupidity was refreshing. Proof that their tribe could win back the meadowlands someday."

"Have you seen those krens since?" Sem shot a quick look at Gundack, probably had thoughts about the amulet shop in Jular Village.

"One of them eventually became my driver." Rheemar shook his head from side to side. "I still can't believe he betrayed me. All those other merchants. Dead. It wasn't like him to do that."

"Did you seal your blood pact," Gundack said, "with him?"

Rheemar's eyebrows knitted together in a single line. He set down his rope and placed his hands behind his back. Yet his eyes focused forward.

"My driver wasn't my blood ally," Rheemar said. "Only an ordinary friend." He glanced skyward. "No, more than ordinary. One time, I slipped while climbing. A sharp rock sliced my calf. Blood spattered everywhere. I couldn't walk. He got me down the mountain. On ropes. On his back. Anyway he could. How could he have betrayed me after all that? I would not have thought it possible. But of course he did, didn't he?"

"I believe so," Gundack said.

Gundack fingered his rope. At least Rheemar had learned a valuable lesson from his experiences. Kan, on the other hand, never would learn from his.

"Do you see this?" Gundack spread a section of worn line across the palms of his friendship hands. "This weak point probably started to develop before you climbed Jular Steeps. It was night when you pulled this rope from my pack. Raiders were attacking. Immediate action was needed. You had no time to examine for defects. You did what you had to do by faith."

Rheemar tossed him the hide pouch of berryroot, his lips pressed together. The sides of his mouth turned down. Gundack extracted a small piece of the crimson tuber and rubbed it against the damaged section of line. He would want to locate the specific worn spot later.

"Don't we all check our ropes regularly," Rheemar said, "to prevent failure when we need them the most?"

"Yes," Gundack said. He slipped the berryroot back into the pouch. Scarlet stained his fingertips. He rubbed the excess on a shallow layer of sand. "But no inspection catches everything. And no repair is perfect. Nor can I liken friendship to links of fibers. Friendship is held together by so much more, yes?"

"But once I climb with a rope," Rheemar said, "I expect to understand the way it stretches under stress."

"You are only a man," Gundack said. "I am only a kren." He let his mouth curve into a smile. "We are allies but withhold knowledge from each other." His friendship hands jerked another section of the line taut between them. "I won't be certain which way you'll stretch, until you freely let me read you."

CHAPTER FOURTEEN

A BRIDE WOULD HAVE COST LESS

A crusty orange growth infested the crevices of jagged black rocks. Gundack crouched near Rheemar at the base of the mountain. Sucker slimes. Not the way they looked on docks. Were the slimes dormant or dangerous? The human fastened his rope to an iron grapnel, a square pack against his back. How prominent the veins in his forearms were, as though narrow blue-gray ropes stretched beneath his skin. Black hairs raised on the backs of the human's hands. Gundack's tongue tingled. He could almost taste Rheemar's tension. The human worried about the orange colonies and the pending climb. Something else troubled him, as well.

Rheemar stood. The grapnel's four tips looked more tapered than Gundack remembered. And no hint of rust edged the shaft. This piece of equipment wasn't from his own pack, wasn't the one the human had used to scale Jular Steeps.

"Did you buy a new set of hooks at Jular Village?" The fingers of Gundack's friendship hand explored the grapnel's cool surface. No pitting or other irregularities. This was well made.

"I salvaged it," Rheemar said, "from my campsite on Jular Plain. It's a good friend."

"The grapnel has been through a fire?" Gundack said.

"Believe me," Rheemar said, "this is a good set of hooks." His fingernail tapped the iron shaft. "No one crafts a grapnel like a mountain kren."

"A mountain kren?" Gundack bent down and clasped the shaft of the grapnel. In the ancient days, the gods had taught the tribe of the bloodstone rings to write words, mine ore and forge metal. Yes, there was the characteristic symbol in the iron—a scroll banded by a ring. A member of Tarr's tribe had made this. "A bride would have cost less."

"It was a gift," Rheemar said. He glanced toward the ground, then straight at Gundack. "Made by my driver's father."

"Father and son," Gundack said. "You should ponder that connection."

"I already have," Rheemar said.

Rheemar called to Sem and offered the grapnel for inspection. The kren rubbed the side of one hook, then another. All their lives would depend on those four hooks. Sem's friendship hand gestured a sign of approval.

Rheemar retrieved the grapnel and tugged at the rope connection. He stared up at the mountain. His tongue rimmed his lips. Rheemar tossed the implement underhand, not the way he had used his sling. The set of hooks glided toward a ledge, pulling the line, like a graceful bird uplifted by wind. The grapnel caught between jagged black rocks above an overhang. Gundack stepped beside Rheemar and yanked the line. The hooks held fast. The human must have learned his skill from a mountain kren, perhaps the driver who had given him this gift. Hopefully, Rheemar had not acquired his sense of honor from the same source.

"Sem should go first." Rheemar patted Gundack's injured battle arm. The wound had closed six days ago. "You might need a hand onto that ledge." He shook his wrists, then stretched his arms, fingers spread, above his head. "I'll go last."

"Should we shinny straight up the rope," Sem said, "or can we use the rock face?"

"For this section," Rheemar said, "you can touch black rock with your heels. Don't let your toe-claws make contact. The crusty slimes will break off and get underneath."

Sem adjusted his hefty backpack and stepped up to the loose hanging line. He clasped the rope, bent one knee toward his chest and rested his heel against vertical black stone. The hide coverings around his feet didn't extend to his claws.

"How close to Tarr's cave," Sem said, "did you actually climb?"

"Not close enough." Rheemar cinched a pack strap around his waist. "I fell between ledges. That's when I sliced my leg. I still don't know why I didn't break every bone in my body."

"No wonder you want to go last," Sem said. "Uh, did your friend know your destination?"

"Of course," Rheemar said. "We attempted the climb on a dare."

"Was this the set of hooks you used?" Gundack said. That father and son idea had merit.

"No," Rheemar said. "After I healed from the accident, my driver's father insisted I learn to kill myself using decent equipment."

Sem scratched the back of his neck, then pulled himself up the rope and off the ground, his back leaning away from the side of the mountain. A shaft of sunlight shone upon his scarlet and green head scales, then disappeared. Clouds gathered in the blue-gray sky.

"My arms feel so good," Sem said. "I've always wanted to wrench them off."

"Watch your claws," Rheemar said. He folded his arms against his chest and tilted his head upward. "This is our strongest rope. I don't want it shredded."

Sem edged upwards. At first, his heels walked against the side of the mountain. Then he swung out, his thick, leathery thighs

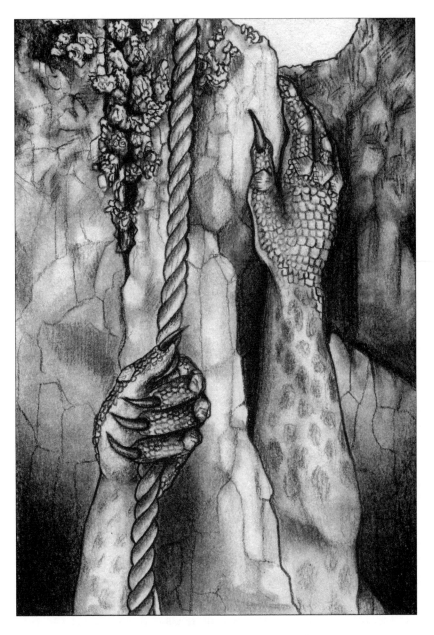

"Orange crusts overflowed a narrow crevice."

hugging the line. His tail, as wide as three fat ropes, shifted this way and that as his sturdy battle arms pulled him skyward. Sem grunted. Finding the right balance while climbing a rope took practice. Not a skill desert krens perfected.

"How many tosses of the grapnel," Gundack said to Rheemar, "before we're above the sucker slimes?"

"Not many." Rheemar shrugged. "Maybe a half dozen."

"I'm not comfortable," Gundack said, "with using your hooks."

"I won't use hooks or a rope I don't choose," Rheemar said. "Not on this mountain. That's just the way things have to be. And by the way, expect traps when we reach the path."

"Poison knives?" Gundack's father had taught him how to conceal blades point-up in sand or dirt.

"And hidden pits," Rheemar said. "Mountain krens told me so one night, five years ago. We'd been relaxing around a campfire, seven or eight of us, and drinking fermented kettlefruit juice. Daring each other to climb to Tharda's Bowl and brew tea. One of my companions even claimed Tarr was his brother-in-law's uncle. I think they all were off guard and told the truth."

Rheemar had gotten drunk with a bunch of mountain krens? Members of Tarr's tribe? Possibly his close family? Even if they hadn't been raiders—had totally despised Tarr's way of life—the human had risked disaster. He could have wound up with a dagger in his back. Or worse. Gundack never would have taken such a chance. But then, he wasn't Rheemar and didn't have the same sort of luck.

Luck. One of the mountain krens in the amulet shop at Jular Village had worn an emerald bloodstone band on his claw finger. Had he been a climbing companion of Rheemar's? Had the human pledged loyalty to a member of Tarr's inner circle?

"What dares did you accept?" Gundack said, "other than climbing to Tarr's cave?"

Gundack's ears flattened against his head. Rheemar gave him a hard look. Then his hazel eyes softened. His shoulders slumped.

"Not the one to sell myself to Tarr."

Rheemar had defended Gundack and his krens during the battle with Tarr's raiders. Risked his life. Gundack's suspicions probably hurt him. Yet Rheemar still feared to extend the palms of his hands, to be read when most vulnerable.

Gundack tilted his head skyward. Sem crawled onto the first ledge now. The rocky outcrop appeared large enough to hold the three of them at once. Gundack stretched out one calf, then the other. His turn to ascend.

The weight of his backpack dragged against his shoulders. Food and water. Bandages and rope. Daggers and spare strips of hide. Had he forgotten anything critical? He curled one claw hand around the dangling rope. Some fibers were rough and others felt smooth. Friendship with Rheemar was like that.

Sem clicked a signal. Gundack pulled himself upward, pressing his heels against the black rock face. Orange crusts overflowed a narrow crevice. He wouldn't rest a foot there. Something pinched within his left battle arm. A sharp pain shot from his wrist to his shoulder. His wound had not fully healed. He would have to depend on his right arm as much as possible.

He dragged his frame higher, leaning one way, then another. His tail shifted. His arms ached. Everything inside of him seemed to push against his skin. The feeling of internal pressure returned. Gundack panted. This would be a long day.

CHAPTER FIFTEEN

ON THIS MOUNTAIN

Icy wind stung his cheeks and nose. Gundack sat on the ledge and drew his knees toward his chest. How many times had Gundack crawled up a section of slime-free rock face or lugged his hulk up the line? His head throbbed. His arms burned. At least this table had room for him and his companions to rest.

Sem's tongue clicked an invitation to move closer. Gundack huddled next to him and Rheemar and listened to the rising wind howl. According to countless stories, the Cave of Spirit Echoes claimed lives. Maybe those unfortunate climbers had succumbed from exhaustion. Even Tarr would have slept for days after this ordeal.

"Can you handle two more ledges before nightfall?" Rheemar's teeth made clicking sounds. Humans sometimes did that when very cold.

"Why do we have to?" Sem's rasps were a cross between growls and groans.

"Do whatever you want," Gundack said. He wedged his friendship hands under his armpits. Maybe he would lose less body heat that way. "I think I've already frozen to death."

"There's a small cave up there. I used it the last time. A couple ledges before I fell."

Gundack's ears pricked. A cave? A good shelter unless inhabited by something large or poisonous. Yet he was so tired. Could he manage two more climbs? He remembered standing watch the night the encampment had burned. He had been exhausted then, too. He had thought about Kan when sleep had enticed him. Had let anger fire his blood and keep him alert. Maybe Gundack should stew about Tarr now. No, he didn't need rage. Besides, focusing on Tarr would invoke mental images he didn't want to see. Concentrating on Kan would bring controllable anger, not enough to affect his judgment.

"My hands are pretty numb." Sem rewound a strip of hide around one claw hand, then clenched and relaxed his fists. "I'm willing to try though."

"How about you?" Rheemar tapped Gundack's back. "Listen. It wasn't as cold up here the last time. I didn't think one moon cycle could make this much difference."

"It's all right," Gundack said. After twenty years of trading expeditions, he should have known better, too. Besides, Gundack usually climbed better in light clothing. And Rheemar had stuffed the ropes and grapnel in their packs several ledges ago. Not much room left over. They couldn't have carried or worn much cold-weather gear. "Let's get going."

Gundack stood. Rheemar rubbed his upper arms, his eyes dull and vacant. Was something wrong?

"Are you all right?" Gundack extended his arm to offer help.

"I think so," Rheemar said, as Gundack pulled him to his feet.

"I bet." Sem patted Rheemar's shoulder. "You're picturing a nice warm cave and a good-looking woman."

"I wish I was," Rheemar said.

What had he meant?

Sem stretched his arms high and his claws gripped the mountainside. He moved upward, slower than a slime crawler. Sem's sense of humor may be lively, but the rest of him had tired.

Gundack's turn. The fingers of his claw hands felt cold, blunt and wooden, as though they belonged to someone dead. He opened and closed them several times to work more blood through his muscles. Some help. Not enough. He reached for the rock but couldn't get a firm grasp. He clapped his hands together. They stung, a sign of feeling. He slapped them against his thighs. He could grip the crevices better now. No crusty orange colonies grew within them. Time to climb.

He bent his knees and sprang upward to get some lift. Pain shot up and down the length of his bad arm as he crawled. Even his good one hurt. Well, nothing to be done but climb, think about Kan and get the misery over with as fast as possible.

Kan. Gundack could still hear the krenling's pained cry for help. Kan, pointed head-first and on his belly, clinging for his life to the face of a steep bluff. That never would have happened if Kan had worn his belly-wrap. But he'd been too ashamed to take off his tunic and robe in front of the other krenlings and wrap his sensitive parts. Then his belly had hurt too much to concentrate on climbing. So what if Kan had blue streaks on his stomach? He should have accepted his deformity, done things the right way and remained alert. A good lesson to remember.

Sem's arm reached down, steadied Gundack and helped him scramble onto the ledge. Gundack panted and his knees scraped rock. A human grunt came from below. Rheemar was on his way. Gundack rose and peered down the mountainside. The top of the human's head emerged from under an overhang. A line of bronze skin divided the two sections of his coarse black hair. His braids wobbled one way, then the other. He canted his head upward. His eyes opened wide but didn't appear focused. Sem and Gundack leaned over and pulled him toward them. The human struggled onto the ledge.

"Give me a moment." Rheemar's chest heaved hard. "To catch my breath."

Gundack had always found it difficult to do work when high in the mountains. Muscles tired before they should. He never could get all the air he desired. This human must feel the same.

Rheemar stood. He stretched one leg behind him then shifted position. He shook both wrists. Then that vacant look returned to his eyes. Did the human have altitude sickness?

"I don't remember this set-up," Rheemar said. "I think we're approaching the cave from a different angle." He blinked his eyes several times, scratched under a shoulder strap and frowned.

"Do you see more sucker slimes?" Sem said.

"No," Rheemar said, "let's keep going."

Icy wind pushed against Gundack's back. Sem dug his curved claws into crevices and edged upward, ropy tail curled against his lower spine. Gundack's sore arm ached as Sem struggled. He could feel his driver's frustration and discomfort. Finally, Sem stood on the next ledge, panting hard. He signaled to Gundack.

Gundack climbed. Pain raced through his arm. What didn't burn, throbbed. He should focus on his actions, not make mistakes. But he needed something to push him. Again Kan.

Fury in Kan's eyes, the angry young kren pounding Zel's chest with the back of his claw hand, just because she'd refused to move. Why hadn't Kan realized she'd found a sand well, a place to get precious water? Seven raps of Zel's spiked tail—even a novice caravan driver knew the code. Gundack had trusted Kan with responsibility and the dishonorable idiot had dared to hurt Zel.

Gundack edged up the next section of rock. Yes, it was easier to take the pain when anger rose within him.

"I know," Kan had said, "I can get work as a boatbuilding apprentice in Nath." How he had begged Gundack to loan him a young sandship lizard to ride to the nearest port city. Why would a desert kren want to build boats? Eutoebi's brother had been so misguided.

Gundack's claws slipped against stone. If only it wasn't so cold. The overhang loomed three kren-heights above him. Once there, the really painful part would begin. Lifting his hulk onto the ledge.

Kan had not returned the young sandship lizard. Even worse, he had never sent one single starstone home to provide for Eutoebi and their elderly father. Better if Kan had been a kren of chalk, stunted and unpigmented. Physically incapable of arduous journeys or defending family and tribe. No one expected much of krens or krenesses of chalk.

Gundack was just below the ledge now. His wounded arm begged for relief. Sem, on his belly, reached down from the overhang. Gundack wasn't close enough. He would have to pull his frame higher and work both arms onto the ledge. If only he could purchase better leverage with his feet.

Blood pounded through Gundack's temples. Pain stabbed his back, shoulders and arms. Maybe if he thought about Eutoebi, about her creamy white belly skin. How he had wanted to stroke her that warm afternoon. She had been stretching to mend a tent flap. But she had pulled down her robe and turned away. That day, she and Gundack had yet to discuss marriage. Touching her stomach would have been dishonorable. Gundack envisioned her above him, calling him, waiting with her four arms extended.

"Take my hand," Sem called, his claw fingers spread. Sem and the top of the ledge looked so close. But if Gundack gripped him wrong, they could slash each other.

"Not yet." Gundack crawled and grunted. His eyes were almost level with the overhang. The ledge was roomy and flat as a table. He had to move left and onto horizontal rock. "Get ready to grab the back of my pack."

Gundack's hands were so numb. Sem reached down. The weight pulling on Gundack's back lessened.

"Got you," Sem said. "Slide two of your elbows up onto the ledge."

Gundack mustered all of his strength to lift himself. Sharp pains ripped through his arm and down his spine. Sem pulled on Gundack's backpack and grunted. Soon Gundack would wiggle onto the overhang. But something was moving, slipping under his elbows. The weight of his body was pulling him backward—downward. Son of a pus worm!

Then Sem clamped Gundack's wrists with his friendship hands. He thrust his battle arms under Gundack's armpits and lifted. Gundack pitched forward. His chest dragged against rock. He was mostly horizontal now and on the ledge. Gundack panted, throbbed and groaned. Safe, at least for now.

"Is he all right?" Rheemar called from below.

"I think so," Sem said.

Gundack turned onto his side. He drew his knees to his chest, then turned enough to push against the ground and kneel.

"Get ready for me," Rheemar shouted.

Gundack stood on wobbly legs and peered over the edge. The human ascended the rock, his clawless hands searching for secure holds. Thank the gods this would be today's last climb. Sem knelt and grabbed Rheemar. Wind flapped the human's robe and pushed his braids forward. Sem drew himself to standing, plucked the human off vertical rock and deposited him on the overhang.

Rheemar rolled onto his back, bare legs bent and eyes glazed, like a dying bug. Twilight's shadows enveloped the ledge and wind increased in intensity. Cave or no cave, this was as far as they could go until morning. Gundack surveyed the ledge, larger than the other ones they had encountered today.

"I hope this is the right place," Rheemar said.

Gundack edged forward with a half-stumble. His legs didn't want to support him. Yet something lay ahead, a curve in the mountainside, he must explore. A black arch stretched between boulders near the far end of the ledge. He squinted. The dark place was not stone. Gundack faced the entrance to a cave.

"Oh, dear Tharda," Rheemar called.

Gundack wheeled around to face the human, battle arms tensed. What was wrong?

"When I close my eyes," Rheemar said, "I see Tarr. He's alive. On this mountain."

"What are you talking about?" Gundack said.

The human, still on his back, groaned. Gray tinged his bronze face, as though he had stopped breathing. Saliva trickled from the corners of his mouth.

CHAPTER SIXTEEN

A DEADLY WORK OF BEAUTY

Gundack peered into the cave. Daylight speckled the gray rock floor, filtering through ethereal silver threads. No, not thread. Silken braids—not single strands—dangled from the high, shadowy ceiling, shifted with each breath of wind. Weavermoss. The handiwork of poisonous web-threaders. This could be a long night, or a very short one.

Bad enough that Rheemar had claimed Tarr was alive and on the mountain. What had the human become, a soothsayer? And now, the shelter they had struggled to reach was inhabited by threaders. Gundack sniffed the dank air and tipped his ears forward. Water dripped. Something rustled. Those deadly insects often congregated by the thousands near water sources in caverns. Tarr or no Tarr, Gundack had better remain wary and take care where he stepped.

A low moan emanated from the darkness ahead. Gundack's ears flattened. His head scales prickled and his skin itched. This potential refuge before him was not the Cave of Spirit Echoes. Tharda's tea bowl balanced on its side far up the mountainside. But the dead had passed this way. Maybe Tarr's spirit, not his living form, roamed this mountain.

"You claimed you could see Tarr." Gundack smelled Rheemar's pungent sweat and turned. "You should have told me to expect web-threaders, too."

"There shouldn't be many," Rheemar said. The human ascended the short incline leading to this cave. The normal color had returned to his face. "There weren't last time."

"Oh?" Gundack scanned the braids of weavermoss. At least fifty nearby. How many more did shadows conceal? "Are you sure this is the same cave you used before?"

"It's dimmer in there than I recall." Rheemar rubbed one shoulder.

"Could be," Sem said from behind the human, "the time of year."

"No," Rheemar said, "this is a different cave. I stood inside the last one without bending over, but I don't think you could have. This ceiling is much higher."

The human took a hesitant step across the threshold. The backs of his hands pushed aside two filamentous braids of weavermoss. He turned toward the right, the outline of his flat nose tinged with daylight. A fluorescent blue insect, half the length of Rheemar's middle finger, plummeted from the cave's ceiling and landed on his forearm. A web-threader. Gundack clicked a warning.

The creature, long and narrow as the fine end of a sewing awl, explored the maze of dark hairs on Rheemar's bronze skin with its twelve legs and tapered head. The human stood motionless. Clearly, he had no intention of flicking the insect away. Not the usual human response. But, then, hadn't Rheemar hung a braided amulet in the entrance to his tent on Jular Plain? He knew how rapidly a startled threader could pulse poison through the injector on its belly.

"Let him get the feel of you," Gundack said, still in the cave's entryway. He opened his eye membranes. How long would it take his pupils to dilate? He must be careful not to smash insects underfoot.

"It probably hasn't met a human before," Sem added.

"I know," Rheemar whispered.

"I thought you went shopping for a new amulet," Sem said.

"I didn't find what I wanted."

The shadows grew sharper now. Gundack's adapting eyes scanned the far wall. A hefty square object, the shape and size of a climber's pack, drew his attention. Who had planned to spend the night here? A mountain kren? Tarr? Had this traveler gone deeper into the cavern to forage for water? Gundack tested the air but sensed no fresh odors of strangers—kren or human.

Web-threaders were protective of their territory. Anyone venturing into inner chambers would not likely return. Rheemar motioned to Gundack and edged toward the object. A half-dozen web-threaders swung seemingly out of nowhere, suspended on braided silk. Their cobalt blue thoraxes shimmered, even in the dim light. They attached to the human's shoulders and arms, like living gems adorning him for decoration. A seventh landed on his head and crawled down the nape of his neck.

"I think this is a travel pack," Rheemar said, with no hint of the anxiety he must have felt. "Our little friends have carpeted the surface pretty well with their silk moss. Looks like they snagged a young ledge lizard in the process. Don't imagine they want their dinner table disturbed."

A clear area lay beyond several dangling ribbons. A suitable place to sleep. Gundack extended his friendship hands, clicking for Sem to remain at the entrance. Sticky ribbons of weavermoss parted like opening curtains, without damage to interlaced strands.

"Maybe they'll loan us this side of the cave," Gundack said. "After all, krens and web-threaders have co-existed in the mountains for a long time."

A web-threader dropped onto the bridge of Gundack's nose and slid down. Tiny legs gripped the fleshy borders of his nostrils. Two eyestalks swiveled, like wet fingers determining the direction of wind. The brilliant insect vibrated four barbed antennae and stared directly into Gundack's crossed eyes. Gundack resisted the impulse to flinch.

A full dose of web-threader poison would cause paralysis. Inability to move a limb—or even to breathe—would result, depending on the injection site. Any rapid movement could trigger a full or partial release. Gundack took slow, shallow breaths and watched sensory appendages oscillate. He could never adapt to living with threaders on a regular basis. Another good reason not to be a mountain kren.

"Let's talk this over," Gundack said, his rasps soft, as though he introduced himself to a young krenling. Web-threaders probably didn't understand Sandthardian. But they might differentiate a benign tone from a threatening one. "We need a place to rest." His friendship hand motioned toward a vacant section of the cave floor. "Would you accommodate us?"

The insect twitched its longest antennae, the one with the silvery barb. The slight but steady pressure of an injector remained relentless against Gundack's nose. Maybe huddling outside all night wouldn't be a bad choice, after all. The wind whistled a reminder. Icy air would cut through their cloaks and drain warmth from their bodies. Shelter was essential.

"Rheemar," Sem said, "maybe you're the problem. That moss-covered pack is probably studded with egg sacks."

Sem clicked for the human to move. Rheemar edged sideways toward Gundack, barely lifting his feet off the rock floor. His hands and wrists arced away from the lateral surface of his thighs. Now

Gundack could read the fear in the human's eyes, smell it in his sweat. One web-threader hopped off Rheemar's shoulder. Another dropped free of his arm. Then the insect on his neck jumped clear and scampered away.

"Was that the last one?" Rheemar whispered. He turned around with care, as though maneuvering bare feet between pieces of broken glass.

"The last one we could see," Sem said. "But one could have crawled into your backpack."

The web-threader on Gundack's nose clung to its perch. The insect's long, thin proboscis probed and tickled. How tempting to brush away the creature and crush that brilliant blue thorax underfoot. Something rustled above him. A shimmering blue army gathered on the ceiling. He purged a slow steady stream of breath through his teeth. He needed to calm his thoughts as well.

The insect dropped from Gundack's nose to his chin. Now the prickly injector pressed there. Gundack's shoulders jerked. An involuntary shudder. Barbed antennae tapped the crevices of his lower lip. If only he could shake his head or bat his chin. Yet, wait. Wasn't this web-threader larger than the ones who had leaped onto Rheemar? Gundack was stockier than Sem and nearly twice the human's height. This insect might be a sort of commander, approaching Gundack, seeing him as the leader. Might this threader be trying to read his intentions in some primitive way?

With a slow, tentative movement, Gundack extended his friendship arms, palms up. Bands of mountain krens had dwelled in caves since the ancient days. This introductory hand position might trigger a web-threader instinct, a memory passed from generation to generation. The prickly sensation on his chin ceased. He sensed the landing of something on rock.

"He's off you," Rheemar said.

"I think," Gundack said, "we're relatively safe right here."

The web-threader scurried across the cave floor and into a crevice. How Gundack's chin and nostrils itched. He could still feel where the threader's sticky feet had clung, where the poison injector had pressed against his skin. He rested one claw hand on Rheemar's forearm.

"You are here to mourn," Gundack said, "and I must fulfill a vow. Perhaps they understand."

Gundack's pack tugged at his shoulders. Time to put it on the floor. An exploring web-threader could have crawled anywhere. He had better not remove his gear without help. He clicked for Sem.

"Check the spade, first," Gundack said, "then around the closure."

"They look clean to me." Sem hefted the pack. The truncated trenching spade clattered as the hide bag thumped the cave floor. "We'll have to search everything well tomorrow morning."

"What do you suppose happened," Rheemar said, "to the owner of that other pack?"

"I doubt we'll ever know," Sem said and grinned. "I suspect threaders gave him a robe he didn't choose."

The human slipped off his own gear bag and glanced around the cave, as though he expected to find a human skeleton dressed in weavermoss. He brushed the side of each hand against the opposite arm.

"That glue on the tips of their feet always makes my skin itch," Rheemar said. "Once I woke up with fifty of those filthy things on me. Didn't dare move. It was all I could manage to keep from screaming or retching. My companions just laughed. Told me the

*"It would not take an army of web–threaders
to overcome a human and two krens."*

weavers admired my braids. I don't know how mountain krens stand it."

"My father," Gundack said, "slept sitting up when in caves. Try draping your arms over your bent knees tonight. Let your head hang forward. He claimed the bugs will stay out of your mouth."

"Never worked that well for me," Rheemar said, "but I'll try again." He scratched the back of his neck. "Besides, our innkeepers didn't give us much room to stretch out."

The human extended his arms above his head and yawned. His stomach gurgled. Probably empty. Men digested food faster than krens did. He had mentioned nothing about hunger, though. Gundack gestured to Sem to push their packs close to Rheemar's. Tonight, they would all sit on the floor, their lower backs against their bags.

Gundack scanned the surroundings. What was that near the cave wall? Something light in color and small. He edged over and picked up two smooth white stones painted with symbols. Pebble dice. The size of those used by krenlings when they played hero games, determined who would be the ancient hero. The dice hadn't been in the cave long. Or maybe threaders wouldn't coat little rocks. No weavermoss carpeted the toy. Who would bring a krenling up this mountain?

"Find something?" Rheemar said.

"Are you sure you saw Tarr in your vision and not his krenling?" Gundack carried the dice over to the human and set them atop his backpack.

"Positive." Rheemar placed the dice in his palm and stared.

"Maybe," Sem said, "this would be a good time for you to explain why you see things with your eyes closed."

"You want to know about my visions?" Rheemar sucked his lower lip. The cave's shadows blended with the dark circles underneath his lusterless eyes. "I think they come from my blood brother."

"Oh?" Gundack had heard claims that could happen. "And how would he know about Tarr's location?"

"Because the raiders know," Rheemar said, emphasizing each word.

"Your blood brother is a raider?" Gundack could hear the anger in his own voice.

"No," Rheemar said. "He's their prisoner."

"Why would Tarr capture your blood brother?" Did Gundack really want the answer to this question?

"To get even with me," Rheemar said. He slipped both hands behind his back. "The man who dares to make friends with mountain krens."

"Shortly before you came to my tent at Jular," Rheemar said, "I meditated and heard a voice inside my head. My blood brother's, I thought, although the rasps sounded strange. The same voice had instructed me to travel to Jular Village, where I sold all my wares, then to Jular Plain. My blood brother said to expect your arrival. That's how I guessed who you were. I have no idea how he, if that was his voice, knew about you."

"Unless the raiders knew." Gundack felt his body stiffen. There was only one way anyone but his drivers could have known he had planned to journey to Jular. Son of a pus worm.

"Never trust a soothsayer who isn't your relative," Gundack said.

Soothsayers, Tarr, Rheemar's story and the krens in the amulet shop were all fragments of a larger truth. And the human still kept his hands behind his back. Gundack would have to read

Rheemar without feeling the pulse of his blood. He must discover the human's truths.

§ § §

Wind moaned beyond the cave and within its hidden recesses. Gundack sat under a blanket on the cold, hard floor. He pulled his cowl tighter around his head and drew his bent knees toward his chest. He was practically back-to-back with his companions, except for the packs separating them. Maybe combined body heat would help keep each other warm. If Tarr were alive and on this mountain, he'd be huddled in a cave, too.

How angry and bitter the northland krens must have felt seven hundred years ago, after eviction to the rugged Divider Mountains. To leave verdant meadows and fast-flowing streams for caves and barren, jagged rocks. How many of the old and sick had fallen to their deaths? How many krenlings, covered with web-threaders, had screamed and thrashed in terror, then succumbed to injected poison? No wonder time had not cooled the anger of Tarr's tribe.

Anger. Interesting how tonight's encounter with web-threaders had temporarily muted Gundack's own bitterness, his hunger for vengeance, his growing compulsion to harm Tarr's family. When he had seen the pebble dice, he had not lusted to tear apart Tarr's krenling. But, then, Talla had been a well of forgiveness. Her soothing spirit must be reaching out to him.

The soft glow of moonlight pooled at the entrance to the cave, like still water in a pond. Eutoebi was forgiving, too. She still loved her brother, regardless of everything he'd done. Eutoebi would be a fine wife and mother. She should be, all full of health and life. Not like her unpigmented friend, Zydra, a kreness of chalk. When Zydra came of age, tribal elders would have to cast dice on behalf of all the tribe's married krens to make a match. The loser would get her for a helper wife, for she would be too fragile to bear healthy krenlings. A talenbar potion would persuade Zydra's future husband to do his duty. Gundack would need no such encouragement with Eutoebi.

Gundack gazed upward, listening to Sem's steady breaths. Silhouettes of three web-threaders swung back and forth in the air, their silk lifelines cloaked by night. They passed between each other, around each other, braiding their threads into strands of silver moss. Did they weave only to catch food? To mark their territory? Or, could such a small being experience exhilaration or joy? A shiver darted down Gundack's spine. It would not take an army of web-threaders to overcome a human and two krens.

"Gundack," Rheemar whispered, "are you awake?"

"As far as I can tell," he replied.

"Have you been watching them braid?"

"Yes," Gundack said.

"How can those wretched creatures do that?" Rheemar said. "Prepare to inject us with poison, then create a work of beauty? We're like that, aren't we? Your kind and mine? Plotting to betray each other while we decorate brass harness bells."

Gundack grunted in agreement. Moonlight gleamed around the braids of weavermoss, spattering the cave floor with shifting, lacy patterns. How perceptive Rheemar could be. For a human. Was he that way because he had traveled with krens? Or, did Rheemar's sensitivity distance him from most men? The web-threaders dodged and danced, wherever instinct carried them. Where would instinct carry Rheemar?

CHAPTER SEVENTEEN

COMBINED HONOR

His feet itched and tingled, as though barbed antennae tickled soles and webbing. Most of all, Gundack's toes begged for a good scratch. His muscles felt stiffer than the shaft of a trenching spade. Oh, to be in his home oasis, sleeping on indigo cushions and nestled next to Eutoebi. He'd napped next to her once on a warm day. Awakened and licked the rim of her ear.

Gundack opened his eyes, still sitting, hunched over his knees. Dawn's light crept into the cave and around weavermoss. The reek of man sweat was strong. Why did human armpits always smell so foul? Gundack yawned and glanced around. Sem clicked a morning greeting. Rheemar sat cross-legged, meditating. Was the human really Gundack's ally? His story last night had sounded convincing. But that soothsayer's prediction had, too. Too bad traitors didn't emit telltale scents of dishonor.

Gundack yawned again. He would stand and stretch, then chase the itch. Something brushed his leg and scampered across the cave's floor.

"Nobody move," Sem said. "One got me. A threader."

Gundack stiffened, his hands nearly touching the ground. A web-threader had injected Sem. Gundack had witnessed threader poisoning once years ago. The victim's leg had bloated like a dead body on a hot day. How could he aid Sem without moving? He was going to have to do something, and fast.

"How bad is it?" Gundack searched the surrounding flat rock for antennae or fluorescent cobalt blue. Nothing obvious. The ceiling was bare, too. The threader that had scooted away—where was the insect now?

"Your chest," Rheemar said, "does it feel crushed?"

"My fingers don't work right," Sem said. "Left claw hand. And everything below the elbow's going numb."

"Bastards," Rheemar muttered, as though parentage would matter to insects. "One of them hopped onto my instep. Gundack, can you take a look at Sem?"

Gundack grunted, then surveyed his own chest, arms and legs, at least the parts he could see. No threaders. He turned and angled onto his knees, placing his battle hands flat on the ground. He pushed himself into a crouch. Dare he move again? No vermin were in his path. He swiveled toward Sem. How would he know the best thing to do?

Gundack extended his friendship arms and inspected the injection site and surrounding skin. Sem's left hand looked larger than the right. His palm had puffed and felt unusually firm. He took rapid breaths, as though he couldn't get enough air. Some poisons turned clawkren blood bright red or deep blue. Only normal chestnut tinged the pale leathery skin around Sem's claws. Gundack pulled back the kren's lower eyelid. The thread-like blood vessels appeared normal. His body wasn't starving for air. Perhaps fear quickened Sem's breaths. He clasped Sem's friendship hand and read the throb of his life pulse.

"What happened?" Gundack said.

"I had a cramp in my tail," Sem said, "and stretched out my arm when I shifted position. I must have startled the insect."

"If so," Gundack said, "the injection would have been instinctive. Containing only a small amount of venom."

An otherwise healthy kren could probably handle a little poison in the arm. And if Gundack could minimize swelling now, webthreader gangrene wouldn't set in later.

"I don't think you got a full dose," Gundack said. "Only a reminder to rise early, leave fast and not return."

"What are we going to do?" Sem's rasp was high-pitched and strained. "I won't be able to haul myself up the mountain, even if I don't carry a pack."

"We better let the wind chill your hand." Gundack raised Sem's arm.

Gundack's throat pinched. He had come so far, was so close to fulfilling his vow to Talla. Yet how could they continue on? He could finish the climb alone. Rheemar probably could lower Sem on a rope between ledges, and unhook the grapnel before each of his own descents. Yet humans had no claws, never crawled headfirst on their bellies down mountains, the way krens did. Rheemar would have to edge down backward by feel. The two would be easy targets for mountain kren or even Tarr, if that vermin were still alive. Leaving Sem on a freezing ledge or with an army of deadly insects was not even a consideration.

"I think," Gundack said, "the next direction we'll all be traveling is down."

"We'll talk outside." Sem struggled to stand, his boxy jaws set in a grimace.

Gundack put his arm around Sem and assisted him out of the cave. Cold wind whipped at cowls. Cloaks flapped this way and that, like wings on a fledgling lizard bird. Morning had mellowed last night's heavy blow, but not enough. Gundack used his body to shield most of Sem's, while holding the poisoned arm high.

"I'll fix a backrest for Sem." Rheemar dragged the three packs from the cave.

The crisp mountain air smelled of sweet cragweed. Cragweed tea. The day of marriages. Three days had passed since he had left Elar and the caravan. If Gundack and Rheemar lowered Sem to the bottom of the mountain, would they have time, supplies and strength to climb back up here? To reach the Cave of Spirit Echoes and return to the Red Sands as planned?

And what if the human had lied last night? He and that soothsayer could both be loyal to Tarr and have conspired. If so, Sem's absence and Tarr's presence would embolden Rheemar.

"The gods." Sem winced and leaned forward, clutching his stomach. "I think they want us to reach Tharda's Bowl."

"What are you talking about?" Gundack again raised his comrade's left battle arm. "We're going back to camp."

"Do you think I have no perception?" Sem burped. "You're planning to lower me to the base of this wretched mountain and climb back up here all over again. That wasn't our plan."

"Sometimes agreements have to change," Rheemar said. He knelt and lifted the bottoms of Sem's cloak, robe and tunic. "I'm going to check your belly." He poked the cream-colored skin in several places and mumbled some incomprehensible words. "Even if the path to Tharda's Bowl were completely safe—which I doubt—we'd have to edge around two hundred meters of crumbling mountainside to get from here to there. What if you fell?" The human patted Sem's stomach, then checked his legs. "I think, with help, you can crawl down the mountainside."

"All of us made a promise," Sem said to Gundack. He pressed his friendship wrists together, the symbol of a binding vow. "Our combined honor depends upon reaching the Cave of Spirit Echoes."

Gundack nodded, stomach muscles clenched. He ran the palms of his claw hands down Sem's arms, comparing them against each other. Swelling in the poisoned hand had not extended beyond the wrist. It probably would later. But, if they could navigate the narrow ledge leading to the path as soon as possible, they might reach a comfortable place to leave Sem for a while. Then Gundack and Rheemar could finish the climb to Tharda's Bowl.

"I'll lead," Rheemar said, "if you both insist on reaching the cave. But I want heavier items transferred out of Sem's pack. Please. Let me carry more for Sem's sake."

How anxious the human's voice sounded. Because he worried something would happen to Gundack and Sem? Or because he wanted to make sure it did? And what if Jardeen were still alive? In the amulet shop, Tarr's krens might have threatened to cut off more than her hand. Rheemar could have accompanied Gundack and Sem on this journey to ensure they failed. Many had become entwined in Gundack's cause. Not an easy task to determine who some of them really hunted—Tarr, Gundack or Rheemar.

"You're thinking too long," Sem said. "It has to be the three of us."

"Then it will," Gundack said. Wind whistled through a lattice of barren rock.

But could Sem hug the cliff and edge sideways with a useless left hand and numb arm? Talla would be as grief-stricken and horrified as Gundack if Sem fell and died—or if Sem died in the Cave of Spirit Echoes, unable to defend himself against Tarr. Sem had purchased gifts of fabric for Talla on every trading journey, had treated her as a sister. Talla's spirit might even hold Gundack responsible for any harm that might come to Sem.

The human opened his own pack and removed a coil of rope. Then he slipped his head and one arm through the center space. The iron grapnel hung against his right hip.

"Listen to me." Rheemar shifted a hefty water skin from Sem's pack to his own. "If a toehold crumbles under my weight, I'll shout for you to stop."

Gundack surveyed the ledge they would have to negotiate. The shelf appeared no wider than the one he'd maneuvered on Jular Steeps. Yet now, he would climb with an overloaded backpack and an injured friend, as well as a potential enemy. What would be the rhythm of the man's pulse, the thoughts behind his eyes? Rheemar might be capable of murdering Sem and stealing Gundack's future with Eutoebi. Right now, though, his eyes filled with warmth and loyalty. Gundack would trust Rheemar for now.

CHAPTER EIGHTEEN

LIKE A WEB-THREADER

The ages had weathered the Mountain of the Dead since the ancient volcanic eruptions. Gundack edged sideways along the mountainside behind Rheemar, his battle arms spread and chest pressed against speckled, gray rock. Little of the black lava surface remained. There wasn't much of this path left, either. He advanced upward, first testing the steep switchback with his bare left toe, then pressing down his heel. The bottom of his cloak flapped in the wind. This foothold was solid. The next one might not be. Time conquered many things.

"Ready to slide your foot?" he said to Sem.

"Ready," Sem said.

Cold wind rushed under Gundack's cloak and robe, even fluttered the pleats in his under-tunic. His right claw hand clutched the left shoulder strap on Sem's backpack, pushing the driver against the mountain as he moved them sideways and up. So far, this maneuver had kept the two of them from blowing away.

Gundack's left foot searched for the next toehold. Already, the webbing between his toes grew numb. Yet hide coverings would have hampered his grip. Bad enough his roomy cloak kept blowing in the way of his claw fingers. If he lost more feeling in his feet, he would have to wrap them somehow.

"How are you two doing?" Rheemar called, his left side halfway around the next bend.

"I'd trade my last starstone," Sem said, "for a place to sit."

Such a quaver in Sem's voice. Gundack's own arms and legs held a burning sensation. He turned his head toward the right, scraping his nose against rough rock.

"I think I see a wider overhang," Rheemar said, "a few switchbacks above." He coughed. "Whatever you do, don't look down."

"Can't even look up," Sem said. His left pupil had drifted toward the bridge of his nose. Paralysis of the eye muscles. Was the webthreader's poison spreading toward Sem's brain? Sem had insisted on continuing. Gundack shouldn't have agreed.

"Can you concentrate on your forward foot?" Gundack said.

"Just barely."

"Get ready for the next step," Gundack said.

Gundack guided Sem around one bend, then another. The kren's left battle arm hung at his side, as useless as a sack of sand sitting on a dune. Gundack slid his own foot to the left. Tiny shards of black rock stung his skin. At least he still had feeling. He glanced down. Such a distance to the valley floor. More than enough to claim his life if he slipped, and to end his dream of marrying Eutoebi.

An icy blow. A narrow ledge. Tribal elders in the early days had carried baskets of incense along this miserable ledge. Where had their grand-krenlings found room to skip and play? Had the wind really stilled so that young ones could pick fragrant cragweed? But all that had happened so long ago. Years crumbled trails. Retold stories often shifted shape. No living being knew all of yesterday's truth. Tomorrow also would hold truth, if they survived.

"Time to step?" Sem said.

"Yes." His mind drifted too much. He would have to be more careful.

"Stop," Rheemar shouted from around a blind bend.

"What's wrong?" Gundack called. "Has the ledge ended?"

"Stay put," Rheemar shouted, "till I say."

A clink of metal broke through the wind's whistle. Rheemar carried a grapnel and coil of rope. He must have cast his hooks. But, if the human had run out of ledge, he would have no maneuvering room.

"How are you doing?" Gundack said to Sem.

"Not," Sem said between sharp breaths, "very well."

Gundack braced Sem against the rock face. Sem. They'd fought raiders together, led each other through blinding sandstorms. Shared so much all these years. Oh, Talla.

The wind carried the sound of a grunt, of sandals pushing against rock. Gundack listened for Rheemar. Was the human climbing his rope? Every muscle in Gundack's body ached, but he held his old ally in place.

"Now," Rheemar shouted. His voice came from the left, but also from above. "Grab the rope."

Gundack turned his head. A line dangled downward, just beyond his left hand. Gundack stretched, curved his longest claw finger around the rope. His tail uncoiled and teased the line into his friendship hand.

"Got it," Gundack said.

"Tie it," Rheemar shouted. "On Sem's pack."

Gundack shifted the rope end to his right side. He must turn his head to face Sem. Rock scraped his cheek and chin. His friendship hand slipped the line under one of Sem's pack straps. He couldn't reach the far strap unless he used his right claw hand.

"Can you clutch the mountainside," Gundack said, "until I count to ten?"

"I'll try," Sem whispered.

"One," Gundack said. He released his grip on Sem. "Two."

He worked the rope, counting, praying. He forced the line underneath the other pack strap at the count of seven, drew it back at the count of nine. The numbers went by so fast. He again held Sem against the mountain.

"Ten," Gundack said. "But I'll need ten more."

"I'll try." Sem's eyelids lowered.

Gundack's tail and right friendship hand held the rope in place. His claw fingers struggled to tie a knot. This would not be the strongest knot, the one he needed. But it was the best he could do. At the count of ten, Sem's body lost tension, his remaining strength fading.

"Get ready," Gundack shouted to Rheemar. "We're coming up." He eased his head back toward the left and looked up. An overhang waited. "Sem, take a deep breath. I'll go first. Then you're going to dig your claws into the mountain and follow me."

"Now," Rheemar called.

Gundack released his grip on Sem, dug four sets of claws into crevices and pulled himself upward. How far could Sem crawl? If he fell, would rope, pack straps and waist cinch all hold? Gundack could almost see the red mark on the line, the weakest point stained with berryroot, fibers pulling apart. Oh, Eutoebi. If only he could live long enough to marry her.

Gundack's arms burned as he lifted himself. How could Sem ever manage? Now Rheemar was only an arm's length away. The human reached down and behind Gundack's shoulders. The weight of the pack dragged less. Gundack's claw hands gripped the overhang. His toes found footholds. He had achieved the ledge.

"Ten," Sem's slurred voice said from below.

The rope attached above the ledge pulled taut. Gundack scrambled to the edge of the overhang. The driver dangled unable to climb, to do anything but grasp the rope with three hands and a tail.

"I'll pull you up," Gundack said.

He eased the rope upward, his back and arms afire. Sem's yellow eyes—both pupils had rolled to a crossed position, not tracking anything at all. Rheemar's footsteps shuffled behind him. Perhaps the human surveyed the grapnel above. Or something else. Then came another clink of metal. Rheemar stepped off the ledge and dangled in air. At least a dozen crimson marks stained the rope supporting him. Rheemar would never use a rope he hadn't chosen. Now he clung to the spare line that had been in his pack, the one most likely to fail.

The human swung in the wind like a web-threader on weavermoss. He dropped to a point even with Sem, then twined and fastened the end of his rope around Sem's waist. Gundack peered downward, around the bend where the ledge they had been walking ended. How small that shelf was. How had Rheemar managed to maneuver the rope coil, toss the grapnel and snag the hooks in a stable location? He must have performed similar feats before. Young mountain krens did many reckless things on dares. Rheemar must have traveled with them for longer than he had admitted. Thank Tharda, he'd learned so much.

"As soon as I'm back on the overhang," Rheemar called, "pull up Sem."

Rheemar shinnied up the rope. Gundack could almost feel the worn sections of line stretch, the grapnel straining to tip and unseat. Yet the ropes held. Rheemar climbed onto the overhang. Now Sem dangled on two ropes.

"Pull together," Rheemar said, "on the count of three. Then one breath and we start the next round."

Gundack counted, leaned into the weight and pulled. The rope stung his skin, as though fibers were sugarthorn. He and Rheemar hauled again and the injured Sem slipped over the lip of the ledge and onto flat rock. One corner of Sem's mouth smiled. The rest sagged and drooled. His chest rose and fell with an even rhythm. Poison had spread to his face, but not to his chest or diaphragm. Now he rested safe thanks to Rheemar's resourcefulness and leadership.

Rope burns discolored Rheemar's palms. Without doubt, the man who had dared to become friends with mountain krens was a desert ally, too. That ought to infuriate Tarr, if he were alive and ever found out. How appropriate for the raider to stew while those from the Red Sands rejoiced.

CHAPTER NINETEEN

PULSES OF FEAR

Sem shivered, his skin cold to Gundack's touch. Gundack inspected the kren's poisoned battle arm. Still puffed up and hard. Cold was supposed to make swelling subside and put web-threader venom to sleep. Where had he first heard that? More likely, the icy wind would kill Sem long before it healed his arm.

Gundack wrapped Sem's shoulders, feet and hands in goat hide. Rheemar pulled their packs together and formed a three-sided windbreak. Sem sat in the middle, as though he rested in a Northman's chair. The angular-jawed kren could smile or frown with his full mouth, now, even shrug his bad shoulder. His left battle hand remained paralyzed, and his elbow wouldn't flex. But the rest of him was putting up a good fight.

"That last bend," Rheemar said. "The pressure of my foot crumbled what was left of the ledge. If I hadn't had a rope ready . . ."

Gundack grunted, turned, and stared at Tharda's Bowl, still far above. Tarr must have hauled his hulk all the way up there early each winter, an impressive feat. If the raider had survived Jular Plateau, he would have sustained serious injuries. Even with help, how could he have managed to return to this mountain and climb?

"Have you had any more visions of Tarr?" Gundack said.

"No," Rheemar said, his first finger rubbing his whiskered chin.

"Too bad," Gundack said. "I'd like to know where that vermin is."

Gundack stood and studied the path ahead, a series of switchbacks cut into the mountainside. The trail appeared wide enough to walk facing forward, even to accommodate two kren feet side-by-side. Yet Gundack's father had often voiced a wise saying: Never trust a path you haven't survived. His father had told him something else, too. Never trust a merchant who won't let you read him when he displays his wares. Rheemar had shown what he had to offer—loyalty and courage—even though he would not permit Gundack to read him at will. At least not in the common kren manner. But Gundack now suspected he knew much of the man's heart.

Sem huddled among the packs, his spotted lips parted, the margin of the inner surface cracked and dry. Rheemar brought a water skin to Sem and coaxed him to drink. Would they really get off the mountain alive? What would happen to Sem if Gundack and Rheemar died in the Cave of Spirit Echoes? No, Gundack mustn't die here in this miserable place. This mountain would not steal his future with Eutoebi, or the lives of his companions.

"One of us," Gundack said to Rheemar, "will have to help Sem climb down."

"I know," Rheemar said, one hand on Sem's shoulder. "I'll stay here with him if you want."

Rheemar reached under his clothing and untied his money pouch. He withdrew the emerald bloodstone bracelet and turned it over in his hands. His first finger dragged along the edge of the carved morning prayer. Rheemar offered the bracelet to Gundack. "If there's a way to find out about Jardeen . . ."

"I can't promise anything." Gundack transferred the jewelry to his starstone pouch.

"You could promise to ask Talla," Rheemar said.

"She might not know," Gundack said, "or be able to communicate with me."

"You brought me this news about Jardeen," Rheemar said. "Promise you'll try."

Gundack rasped a grumble. He dug out two sheathed silver daggers, the one from his father to be given to one of Gundack's own sons. Perhaps the other Gundack should give to this son of a Northman who sought entry into the family of kren. He secured the two daggers on his sash, then cradled one friendship hand around the human's tense jaw. Rheemar longed to accompany him.

"Watch for my signal," Gundack said. "If I face only spirits when I reach Tharda's Bowl, I'll chance it alone. If I smell mountain krens, I'll need your help."

The human looked down, as though counting specks of dust. Gundack turned and followed the path up the mountainside, stopping every few steps to crouch and prod the ground in front of him with his short trenching spade. A soft spot, then the exposed tip of a metal blade, probably coated with poison. A dozen more steps brought him to a similar trap. Tarr, dead or alive, wished to discourage visitors.

The angle of the path steepened. How easy it was to ascend without a heavy pack, even at this altitude. A pile of dry brush blocked the next bend. A camouflaged pit? Gundack pushed his trenching spade through the mound. He shoved the dry brush aside to reveal the hazard. Yes, a dangerous cavity lay in wait for the unwary.

Gundack progressed switchback by switchback, the wind increasing and carrying a faint putrid odor. Stinkwood. A sign of mountain krens and trouble. Tharda's Bowl sat maybe four switchbacks above him. Gundack leaned into the upward climb. Wind hit the side of his face. He no longer squatted to prod the ground with his trenching spade. The path had grown quite steep. Twisted barbed branches fanned out from low, thick trunks rooted in the mountainside. Gray-green leaves with curled edges clung between thorns. A rancid smell traveled on a gust, an unfamiliar variety of stinkwood. Perhaps the altitude had deformed its leaves and stunted its growth. Or, maybe, a force from the Cave of Spirit Echoes had changed the natural shape of the bush.

Saliva dripped from Gundack's mouth. He panted and ascended around the next bend. Dust stung his eyes. He blinked and squinted, letting his translucent membranes slide back and forth across his eyes until the burning subsided. The inner curve of Tharda's tea bowl loomed ahead, the rust-colored formation looking like a giant drinking vessel. He couldn't see the cave's entrance from here though he soon would.

The foul smell of stinkwood intensified far more than he had expected. Gundack's ears flattened against his head and the base of his tail throbbed. He tightened his claw hand around his trenching spade. His friendship hand reached under his cloak and felt for the hilt of his dagger. Something awaited him in this cave. And it was more likely to be alive than dead.

Gundack picked up several small stones, the size of pebble dice. He cast one against the inner lip of Tharda's Bowl. No unusual sound followed, just a weak thump. He moved closer. The opening into the cave appeared, a separation between two jagged black sheets of rock, wide enough for him to pass. Natural light within the cave would be dim. He cast the second rock near the opening. Still no suspicious sounds. The third stone sailed between the entrance rocks and disappeared. Did he hear a soft rasp? A kreness or krenling noise?

Maybe Tarr had not wintered alone in the outer chamber to the

Cave of Spirit Echoes. Family members might have joined him. Perhaps a wife. A young daughter or son who played the hero's game with pebble dice. The trip up this mountain had been difficult for Gundack, but mountain krens were experienced climbers. Even now, family members could be waiting for Tarr to join them, wondering why he hadn't arrived. Unless he had arrived.

Gundack glanced back down the mountainside. Rheemar stood in the distance, next to the packs and Sem. How small the human was, yet straight and attentive, watching Gundack's every move. Caring for Sem.

Gundack raised his claw hands, forearms crossed, a silent signal to approach with extreme caution. Rheemar returned the signal. Gundack turned back toward the opening behind Tharda's Bowl. Yes, he caught the smell of excrement. Krens must be up here.

Gundack moved closer and inhaled with quiet breaths, analyzing the enemy's scent. If his enemies had recently been in the entry chamber, their foul breath would still hang in that air and Gundack would notice. Instead, the odor of excrement prevailed. And not just ordinary droppings. The acrid reek from urine sludge. But only an elderly or dying kren, one who was severely dehydrated, excreted pasty urine. What mountain kren would bring one nearing death here? No custom supported such an action.

Gundack pressed his frame against the slab of jagged rock. From this position, the wind blowing into the cave would carry less of his scent. Then the crunch of gravel announced Rheemar's approach on a switchback below. He clicked for the human to hold. Those inside the cave probably had heard the noise or surmised visitors. And they didn't know his code. They didn't know who he had signaled or how many. The crunching stopped, replaced by a softer sound.

Gundack tipped his ears forward. Rheemar gathered stones for his sling.

But what sound emanated from the cave? A rustle. No, more of a drone. The familiar noise tensed Gundack's every muscle. Fluorescent cobalt blue filled his mind. Pulses of fear shot down his spine and exploded throughout his entire body. Web-threaders.

VOWS

AND PROPHECY

CHAPTER TWENTY

WHERE IS HONOR?

Gundack stepped into the cave, his shadow dividing the rectangle of daylight on the entryway floor. Odors of excrement and rot grew strong. Pending death. No wonder the smell of kren had been difficult to discern outside. A torch glowed from the rear of the chamber. His protective eye membranes slid open, and he scanned the cavern's dim recesses. No weavermoss dangled from the high ceiling. The rustling web-threaders must reside deeper inside the mountain.

The torchlight held steady, casting modest luminance toward something lying on the floor. Something with legs and arms. A body. Gundack moved closer. The body's chest rose and fell under a black tunic. Notched ears drooped at angles. A mountain kren. Fluorescent orange slime and black mucous oozed from beneath lusterless triangular head scales. A sucker slime colony flourished. This kren would be dead by the next moon cycle.

Rushing air moaned from hidden tunnels in the rock. Who had brought this pathetic creature here? When? And why? Gundack blinked, his eyes adapting to the low light. He examined the body. A filthy strip of linen wrapped one of the kren's fingers. No, the cloth had been wound around a band. An unusually wide ring hung from the kren's bony finger, a finger with yellowed claws. The band was as green as ledge lizard blood and flecked with chestnut hues and amber. Emerald bloodstone. Gundack's breath caught in his chest. Tarr. But Tarr had plunged down a deep hole on Jular Plateau. He should still be there.

Gundack took a closer look at the head scales. Yellow tinged, like the claws, the way Tarr's had been. And this mountain kren's frame, although emaciated, was tall. Dull brown blotches spotted his flat nose. This was Tarr. Rheemar had been right. Gundack crouched, almost unable to breathe. Tarr. His very presence in this sacred place—the entry chamber to the Cave of Spirit Echoes—defiled the dead.

Gundack studied the kren's hollow cheeks, rigid grimace and downward slant to his eyes. A pressure built within Gundack with each breath the dying kren drew. This was Tarr and the vermin lay in peace. No agony. No terror. Just sleeping. Yes, he had sustained massive injuries. But, now, in the mountain where Talla's spirit rested, this son of a pus worm slept like a newborn krenling. What right had he to be so comfortable? He deserved to have his guts ripped out. To be buried alive in a pit of sand.

Images of Talla flared in Gundack's mind. Her mutilated body. Chestnut blood pouring from mangled green and brown flesh. His memory of her. No transcendent perception. But the source of the images made no difference. She deserved justice. Something—anything—more than she had received. Gundack's heart thudded. His temples throbbed. Rage shot from his head to his toes. His claws pressed against the sleeping kren's belly, dug through cloth and into unresponsive flesh. Warm chestnut blood spurted upward and coated Gundack's hand, his arm, his very soul. Gundack roared.

"No," a squeaky, high-pitched voice shouted. "Leave my father alone."

Gundack pivoted, blood dripping from his claws. A small figure darted past him. A krenling. The young one threw itself across Tarr's chest and stomach. Tarr's offspring. The progeny of a murderer destined to grow up and lead raiders or breed more of them. Blood for blood. Death for death. Krenling and father must die together.

Gundack dug his claw-tips into the krenling's shoulders. The little one screamed, jerked away and shriveled back against his father's still form, small hands clutching the raider's black tunic. Dark chestnut blood oozed through the youth's gray robe. Tiny ears flattened against the sides of his head, no notches having yet formed in the ear tips. This krenling couldn't be more than six or seven years old. Hardly more than a baby. And his skin was as white as Zydra's, Eutoebi's dear chalk friend, with a few pale pink and green markings. Dear Tharda, this was a helpless krenling of chalk, the one Tarr had held in his thoughts on Jular Plateau. This krenling would never lead armies, probably never produce offspring. Rage had awakened a disgusting monster in Gundack.

Talla would be horrified to see him claw a little one. Eutoebi, too. When the time came for Gundack and Eutoebi to read each other on the day of marriages, she would know this dishonor. And what if infection set in? If the chalk died? Gundack pulled back from the small white form, tore off his cloak and pressed the cloth against the krenling's wounds. He would need pus worms. Where would Gundack find any up here? Rheemar had traveled with mountain krens and would know where to search. Gundack reached out to Tarr's son, to carry him outside. A small arm thrashed against his, and the cave filled with a vibrating wail.

"Forgive me," Gundack whispered, stepping away. "I won't hurt you again. It's all right."

"Oh, dear Tharda," a kreness rasped.

Gundack turned toward the shadowy entrance to a side chamber. The kreness stood small and erect. A sky blue robe draped her stocky tan and pale green body. Her family hands, the female equivalent of claw hands, shielded her mouth. Terror pushed up both sets of her eyelids and flashed across her golden pupils.

"How dare you," she shouted. She rushed over and lifted the krenling off Tarr, her body shuddering. "Where is your honor?"

Blood drenched the front of the little gray robe. She removed the sopping garment and inspected the young one. The blood had come from his father. Then she knelt, slipped off her own robe and pressed the fabric against Tarr's bloody abdomen. Her tight undertunic revealed the rounded contours of sturdy hips. The krenling of chalk hid behind her, four small hands grasping her bare lower leg. Her ivory belly skin showed as she leaned over Tarr's comatose frame. The raider would never stroke that sensuous belly again.

The krenling whimpered. He must be Tarr's, but how? How could the powerful leader of mountain krens have sired this poor creature? A punishment from the gods? Unpigmented female krenlings, such as Zydra, frequently grew to adulthood, could weave rugs and be helper wives. But male krenlings of chalk almost always expired before age seven. Their intestines blocked, bloated and burst. Or a simple krenling disease advanced at an unstoppable pace. Both were horrible deaths. Here, tribal elders didn't allow such male krenlings to live past the first days of infancy. That was the mountain kren way. Perhaps he had been born looking healthy enough to survive.

"I'm sorry I hurt your son," Gundack said. "He caught my rage. Tarr murdered my wife. My only dealings should have been with him."

"Keep your apologies and your pity." The corners of her mouth

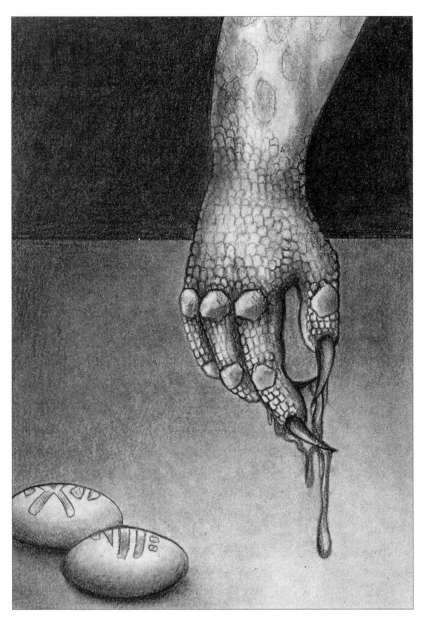

"Rage had awakened a disgusting monster in Gundack."

curled into a scowl. "What good will they do me or my son now, Gundack of the Red Sands?"

"You know who I am?" Gundack said.

"They warned me you would come, when they brought him up here." The kreness turned her head away from Tarr and the krenling, and spat on the cave's floor.

"You know what I must do before I leave." Tribal law permitted him to bury the breathing Tarr in sand, or in the pulverized black lava the kreness had used to keep him clean. "I won't force you or the krenling to watch."

"Revenge," she said. "Violence." She canted her head, golden eyes bright as flames. "What do you—or Tarr—know about anything important? What will you offer when vengeance swallows the land?"

"He slashed my Talla to shreds," Gundack said. The heat of anger again rose within him, even as her words tugged at a memory.

"What does it matter anymore? What harm can he do ever again? That human you travel with killed my two brothers when they slid down ropes to your camp on Jular Plateau. My husband's warriors told me. How could Rheemar, the closest friend of Yender, have done that?"

Rheemar and Yender. The human and Tarr's younger brother. That explained so much. So many secrets. So much to hide. And what did this kreness expect? The very linen robes she and the krenling wore probably had belonged to others, had been stolen either from the living or the murdered.

"You must understand," Gundack said.

"Leave us alone." The kreness stood, her family hands clenched. "I have grief enough."

"'I' must make peace with my wife's spirit," Gundack said. "I promised justice."

"We all make vows." The kreness raised her head high and lifted the naked krenling into her family arms. "I promised my husband loyalty, and our son, life."

He glanced down at Tarr. The ring. Yes, he still had to take care of the band.

"Leave him," the kreness called out, as though reading his mind.

"I need Tarr's ring," Gundack said.

"That ring isn't yours," the kreness said. "It should go to my son, the light of my world, my gift from Tharda."

"If the spirits want your son to have the ring," Gundack said, "they'll return it to him."

Gundack moved to Tarr, crouched and pulled the broad emerald bloodstone band off the bony claw finger. The jewelry slipped onto Gundack's finger with ease. The hand twitched, an unexpected motion. A soft rasp, a rattling whisper came from Tarr. Gundack's muscles tensed. He studied the raider's emaciated face. Eyes remained closed but those spotted lips moved.

"Son," Tarr whispered. "My son. Chosen. Heroes arise."

Tarr's lips stilled. What was this talk about heroes? A delirious mind? He glanced over at the kreness. She attended her son's wounds with herbs. Nothing else. She must not have heard her husband speak. Or had he really spoken? As if Tarr sensed Gundack's question, the dying raider's eyes opened and glowed with life, however brief. The krenling of chalk floated in an image in Gundack's mind.

"Tharda's light," Tarr mumbled. "My son."

The eyes closed. Tarr's breathing dropped into a low rhythm.

Gundack stood and stumbled a step back. He turned to see the kreness and krenling staring at him. All seemed so strange. Words traveled across his mind like ledge lizards panicking in the presence of a predator. What were all these cryptic allusions? Why did they haunt him?

"I will cast this ring into the deep cavern," Gundack said to Tarr's wife, "where Father Sun's tail once plunged."

"The deep cavern?" Her spotted lips formed an odd smile in the torchlight. She pointed toward a jagged crevice in the rear of the chamber. "In the Cave of Spirit Echoes?"

"Yes," Gundack whispered.

"Then you're welcome to the ring," she said, folding her friendship arms around her son. Her voice held a lilt of contempt. "And, if you manage to survive the Cave of Spirit Echoes, you may do what you will with Tarr. With all three of us."

"Then we have both made promises," Gundack said. "See that you honor your word and the spirits' decision."

The rustle of web-threaders swelled and echoed, producing triple drones. They waited for him, the spirits. They beckoned through the rubbing of countless tiny legs and the vibrations of antennae—the threaders' bodies. Gundack could feel the pressure of their injectors against his skin. Oh, Talla. Tarr's kreness had no plans to harm Gundack herself. She was offering him to the threaders and the spirits of the cave.

CHAPTER TWENTY-ONE

VENGEANCE SWALLOWS THE LAND

The rustle and drone swelled, echoed and reechoed in Gundack's ears, drowning out all else at the entrance to the Cave of Spirit Echoes. Thousands—tens of thousands—of fluorescent blue bodies shimmered on the ceiling, walls and floor. Silver garlands of braided weavermoss dangled everywhere, like vines in an old northland forest. They wisped and fluttered, captives of playful air currents, as though enticing web-threaders to ride. How could he pass through this pulsing mass of insects and reach the ancient cavern where the sun's tail had cooled? All it would take was one sting, a single injection of venom to end his quest, his life and family line.

Facing this manner of death was the weakest point on his life's rope so far. Yet honor spoke within him, above the deafening drones and echoes of rattling insect mandibles, rubbing legs and quivering antennae. He must carry Tarr's emerald bloodstone band to the cavern's edge, offer the ring into the ancient cavern, and seek Talla's blessing to marry Eutoebi. If, by some miracle, he survived, he could then return to the Red Desert and his future. He looked out over cracked, uneven ground to the brink of the Cave of Spirit Echoes, a destination he must reach, a journey he must survive.

Gundack blinked. Little clouds of dust hovered near the ground inside the Cave of Spirit Echoes. Dark puffs swirled up from the floor, as though the mountain breathed. Nothing shimmered within those swirls. Might tiny air vents stud parts of the cave floor? Had not his father told him something important about entering this sacred place? Yes, once inside the cave, follow the breath of the spirits.

His eyes tracked the pattern of dust swirls leading toward the cavern's center. If he could walk on the balls of his feet, place them only where he felt the air flow, where no threaders settled, he might have a chance. Some hope of surviving, attaining his dream. Gundack felt the pressure of Tarr's ring on his middle claw finger. Oh, Talla.

Yesterday, when Gundack had entered that other cave, a threader had perched upon his nose. Gundack had extended his friendship arms, palms up. He had opened his inner self to be read. What if he did so again? He rested his battle arms against his sides and closed his translucent eye membranes. Now antennae wouldn't brush the most sensitive parts of his eyes and make him flinch. He reached his friendship arms out as an invitation to touch his thoughts. Then he lifted one foot and moved his leg forward.

The cavern floor exhaled against his heel and toes. Web-threaders swarmed from the cavern's ceiling, swung out from jagged black walls and found perch on his body. Insects coated his arms, legs, chest and face. They clung to his lips and throbbed within his ears. Hundreds of injector tips pressed against his skin. How easy it would be to scream, to thrash. The poison would work fast. He would not have to suffer long.

No. Weakness must not overcome him and take away his honor. He must keep his promises to Talla, Eutoebi and himself. And he must ask about Jardeen. Rheemar had divided loyalties, but had dangled from a spare line and saved Sem's life. The human had faced the weak points on that rope rather than forsake his commitment and sacrifice honor. Gundack owed Rheemar this much and more.

Gundack took another step and then again. How odd, the way threaders hadn't populated the entry chamber to this cave, the haven where Tarr lay. Not a single one perched upon the raider's body. How empty Tarr's expression had been, even when he had whispered about his son and heroes. Could the web-threaders tell he could do no more harm? Did it matter to Talla—to anyone dead—if the raider lived or died? The krenling had been brave to call out, to shield his father the only way he could. How fortunate that Gundack had not inflicted serious wounds. Another breath of air hit his foot, prompting another step. The din of the threaders seemed so soothing now, as though he had taken a potion. The clinging, oscillating mass of blue bodies poured from a distant, hazy dream. They nurtured such peaceful thoughts.

Had Tharda walked with the web-threaders in ancient times, when the God of Wind had imprisoned her underground? Had the relationship between gods and threaders begun there? But he was no god or even a hero. He was only Gundack of the Red Sands, a trader and ordinary kren clinging to threads of honor, the way threaders clung to weavermoss.

How difficult it was to see anything but the fluorescent mass around him and the forest of hanging, dancing silk. A pool of blackness stretched across the ground in front of his feet. He stepped again, this time his toes found no support as his heel landed. A rush of warm air brushed his face, bringing an odor of sulfur. He shifted his weight to his heels. He had reached the brink of the ancient cavern.

He bent his head forward and stared downward into nothingness. A sick feeling washed through his stomach. This must be the crater to the center of Thard, where Father Sun's tail slept. He had almost stepped into the entrance to the subterranean cavern. He had nearly fallen into the realm of the God of Thieves. Now he must prepare to offer the symbol of his triumph over Tarr to Talla, the ancient heroes and the gods. They had given him victory. The bloodstone band belonged to them.

He concentrated, relaxing the barriers to his thoughts and allowing the layers of insects to read his needs. He pointed his claw finger, the one holding Tarr's ring, downward, careful not to startle the threaders.

"Oh, Talla," he whispered. "Always so perceptive, you know my heart already. Let me return to Eutoebi. For whatever time I have left."

His eyes closed as he pictured Talla and Eutoebi side by side in a cloud of red sand, their scarlet robes blown by mystic wind. Each was such a deep well of love and forgiveness, of commitment to family and tribe. More alike than different, each with qualities he now found within himself, flowing to him as though air to be inhaled. As though Talla offered him enduring guidance and Eutoebi opportunities to bring forth love. Now one more matter needed attention. His obligation to the human. Gundack's eyelids raised.

"Dearest Talla," he whispered into the surrounding calmness. "Please tell Rheemar if his sister still lives."

He inhaled again. The moment for the offering had arrived. Gundack eased the ring to the base of his claw. The threaders on his fingers shifted out of the way. The fluorescence of the insects' bodies caught the amber flecks in the bloodstone. Those specks glimmered, as starstones would, the starstones he would offer Eutoebi to be his bride.

The ring slipped along his long curved claw. At the angled edge, the band canted over the pointed tip and tumbled down into the void. Tiny sparkles scattered. A threader riding a silvery strand followed the offering into the blackness. Gratitude warmed Gundack.

He had completed his task, what he had vowed. His heart pounded with those of ten thousand web-threaders. If the threaders took him now, he could fall with honor. Yet Eutoebi waited for his return. Sem needed help down the mountainside. Even Rheemar sought something from him. Guidance and acceptance among the desert kren. All within his power, within the force of his being—strengths he had.

Gundack pivoted, shifting his tail in the air. He set the ball of his foot against the tickle of the spirits' breath and stepped again. The opening to the outer chamber loomed ahead. This journey would need focus. Yet he felt assured of reaching his destination. Each destination in turn.

§   §   §

The entry cave's dim light framed three silhouettes just beyond the archway in front of him. Tarr's wife. The others were shorter. Two krenlings. No, one of the figures was Rheemar. The human must have grown concerned for Gundack's safety to come here now. The absence of Yender must have relieved him. How foolish, all that secret keeping. Openness, not concealment, forged friendship and trust among clawkren. The young man had much to learn. Gundack would help him now that he'd been released from the grip of his hatred for Tarr. Even his resentment against Kan burned with a dull flame. Such inner peace. How beautiful the music of the web-threaders sounded, as pleasing as the tiny brass bells on the harnesses of his sandship lizards.

The last air vent lay ahead. The final step would be a wide one, into the outer chamber of the cave where Tarr slept. Would the web-threaders stay with Gundack? One threader dropped off and scampered away. Poison him? Another followed. Was he worthy to live? Their decision. A third swung toward a braid of weavermoss and vanished. Gundack stood, controlling every rise and fall of his chest, the pressure of injectors against his skin diminishing. Finally, only a single web-threader remained.

The insect, large and blue, grasped his nose. A silvery barb adorned the threader's longest antennae, as with the insect in the lower cave. Might the two be one and the same?

"Step onto my hand," Gundack whispered and closed his eyes. Sticky feet brushed his friendship palm. Barbed antennae probed.

"Read me," Gundack said.

The heat of a thousand angers flushed through him. The warmth of love followed. Did the spirit of an ancient hero inhabit this web-threader? Brilliance flared behind Gundack's closed eyelids within the space where thoughts dwelled. *Tharda's white light shall give strength to the least of us if vengeance swallows the land.* Part of a timeless clawkren saying about calling forth heroes. *Vengeance swallows the land.* One of Tarr's thoughts on Jular Plateau.

Gundack opened his eyes. The insect slid from his hand onto a hanging braid of weavermoss, scampered upward and vanished into the throbbing cobalt blue mass. The light must have come from the threader, a message carried from Tharda. Hate fostered violence while her beam brought forgiveness. The time had come to put all anger behind him and return to the Red Desert, to the life and beliefs the gods had prescribed long ago. He needed to release vengeance from his heart and from his beliefs.

Gundack stepped into the entry chamber of the cave. To his

left, the sleeping Tarr smelled of stinkwood and urine paste. Drool slid from the corner of his mouth. The kreness clutched her frail son against her and stared straight at Rheemar, her golden eyes lusterless and cold. Rheemar gripped the hilt of his silver dagger, his face betraying lust for vengeance.

Gundack could feel the kreness's fear, her compulsion to bolt by him, to throw herself and the krenling onto the milling mass of threaders. An easy death. But she had once promised her husband loyalty and her son, life. Her inner strength to fulfill those obligations had failed her.

"Ask for Tharda's blessing," he whispered to her. "Look to her as I have done, to fulfill your vows."

Gundack retrieved his blood-stained cloak from the cave floor. Long strides carried him toward daylight and the curve of Tharda's Bowl—the way out, the way back to Sem and home to Eutoebi. He could feel the pull of the light.

"Tarr still lives," Rheemar shouted. His voice held such disbelief. "You cannot leave him like this. Only you have the right to end his life here and now."

"Where is your honor?" Gundack turned to Rheemar and gestured toward the kreness and krenling.

"Where are you going?" Rheemar called.

Gundack clicked for the human to follow him, walked through the entry portal and headed down the mountainside. Far better to bury hatred than living flesh.

"To bury Tarr," Gundack called back, "alive."

CHAPTER TWENTY-TWO

SHADOWS ON THE DUNES

Gundack climbed down the steep path from Tharda's Bowl, maneuvering his way around jagged black rocks. The cave. Tarr's warm blood on his claws. The shimmering mass of web-threaders. The golden-eyed kreness filled with such poison. Particularly when she tracked Rheemar. And the chalk krenling Tarr believed was chosen, perhaps by Tharda. Time to evict dark images burrowed into his soul. This matter of vengeance against Tarr and his family had ended. Rheemar craved kren acceptance but valued petty intrigue instead of open communication. Gundack would not succumb to Rheemar's state of mind or what he wanted to happen. He would not let anger flare again. Not against Tarr or Kan or even Rheemar.

"Where are you going?" Rheemar shouted from behind Gundack. "Tarr murdered your wife, mutilated my sister, and you walked out and left him alive. You insult my honor and walk away?"

"Who are you to say such words?" Gundack edged around a knife trap, cold wind pushing against his back, then turned. "You traveled with Yender and didn't tell me. After you made a blood pact with a desert kren. A member of my tribe. You are driven by secrets and dark emotion. This is the honor you pursue?"

"What in Tharda's name," Rheemar said, "did she tell you in there?"

"Enough," Gundack said. "If you're not careful, you're going to find yourself buried alive in sand. And I want no part of such dishonor."

"You don't think I know that?" Rheemar said. "At least let me catch up with you."

Rheemar's footsteps scuffled behind Gundack. Gundack shortened his strides. He would try again with the human.

"You want to read me," Rheemar said. "That's what you're after. You want to learn who my blood brother is. Make sure he's not one of Tarr's kin. Well, I won't let you do that."

"Reading you," Gundack said, "would only reawaken annoying memories." He looked back over his shoulder. "I have a wife to wed."

"You're telling me I'm annoying?" Rheemar's youthful impatience showed in tone and stance. "After all we've just been through together? After I dangled on that rope and saved Sem's hide? My gods! I deserve some respect."

"Have you forgotten the bracelet?" Gundack said, his voice even. "Jardeen's hand? Tarr did that and you're an ally of Yender. My tribe cherishes family and honor above all else."

Rheemar leaped straight across the knife pit, then strode to Gundack. He drew himself to his full height, the top of his hairy scalp level with the bottom of Gundack's rib cage. He tilted his head upward, his steady clear eyes blazing with defiance.

"Yender and I traveled together for five years, much to his family's dismay." The human's forehead flushed, darkening his bronze skin. "Tarr captured and mutilated Jardeen in retaliation."

"Mountain krens," Gundack said, "have despised humans for seven hundred years. Raided their villages. Sold their women and children into slavery. What possible force of Tharda could have forged such a warped alliance? Tell me another story. Tarr and his vermin threatened and bought you. The way Tarr bought your driver. Or were you too young to understand what was happening?"

"How dare you say that." Rheemar stepped back. "We were young, not ignorant. We didn't want the lives our families had chosen for us. We needed to search for something. Find something." Pain filled his eyes. "Maybe just ourselves."

Gundack breathed in the human's scent, could feel him dangling on another sort of rope, one with many weak points. How much Rheemar was like Kan, yet how different. No, the same. Gundack had expected more from them both. Particularly this one, who had shown so much promise. Still had so much potential.

"At Jular Steeps," Gundack said, "did you kill krens you knew?"

"Yes." Rheemar closed his eyes. "It was as though the stones pelted my own chest and throat. But Tarr had sent them to kill me. Yender confirmed that later. He took me aside, in Jular Village, while you and Sem purchased kettlefruit and nuts. He warned me. His family had forced him into an oath of vengeance. We held each other, like frightened krenlings, in the amulet shop, knowing that, the next time we met, we would be in combat. Then he left with one of his cousins who had fought us at Jular Plateau."

"You've misled me before," Gundack said with a calmness he knew he must use. "I want to know you when you have nothing to hide."

Gundack's claw hands enveloped the human's shoulders. The odor of human sweat was strong, but no smell of fear. Rheemar's body may be vulnerable. His mind was not. He was all defiance and anger. Gundack released him.

"So be it," Gundack said.

"Mountain krens have an expression," Rheemar said. "Shadows

on the dunes. When they venture into the desert, raiders pray the dunes will hide even their shadows. Tarr's wife whispered that saying while she watched you walk into the Cave of Spirit Echoes. She didn't think I could hear. Yender's up to something. I can feel it. He's headed for the Red Desert. That's the only reason he wouldn't have been with Tarr."

"Tarr lies near death," Gundack said. "Yender knows that and would not stay while the kreness believes otherwise. It is not mountain kren custom."

"You've got to believe me," Rheemar said. "I know how Yender thinks. Please trust me one more time."

Gundack clenched his fists, then relaxed them. Did Rheemar speak the truth? If so, Yender was the next Tarr. A mutilated young kreness. Dried pools of chestnut blood. Once, Gundack had returned to an encampment and found Talla that way. Oh, dear Tharda. An image of Eutoebi's dark eyes hung in his mind, then shattered like thin glass dropped upon stone. If this could happen, if there was any possibility, he had to trust Rheemar.

"If Yender faced me in battle," Gundack said, "who would you try to kill?"

"I don't know," Rheemar said. "But if I had to slay you, I'd kill myself."

A strange answer. Rheemar still quaked with dark emotion. The human held too many secrets.

"I'm traveling with you," Rheemar said, "to your home oasis. My blood brother will be with Yender now, wherever Yender goes. I've got to help him. And you and your tribe may need a slinger."

"So we travel as friends," Gundack said, "and potential enemies."

"Yes," Rheemar said and bowed his head.

"We better head toward Sem," Gundack said.

Gundack moved down the winding switchback, listening to the human's footsteps following him. A sick feeling washed through him. Rheemar had once said something to him about how consequences filled his life. Those consequences now filled more lives.

"I think Jardeen is all right," Rheemar said in a low tone. "I forgot to mention. In Tarr's cave, I had a clouded vision of a woman with long black hair."

Gundack negotiated a curve in the steep trail and glanced back toward the human. Rheemar rubbed his shoulder, fingering the robe Gundack had given him.

"Thank you for asking Talla," Rheemar said. "You're free from your obligation to me."

Gundack grunted. He had learned much from this pilgrimage. Different obligations bound him to Rheemar now.

"What will you say to the others about Tarr?" Rheemar asked.

Gundack turned back toward the cave's entrance. Tarr's wife and krenling watched from the edge of Tharda's Bowl. Bright sunshine framed the little one. The kreness believed her son was Tharda's gift, her light. Perhaps Tarr had, too.

"There was a kren up there," Gundack said. "Not Tarr. I killed Tarr on Jular Plateau."

CHAPTER TWENTY-THREE

DESIRE WAS ENOUGH

Pink streaks tarried in the pale cobalt blue sky. Ghostly outlines of Tharda's twin moons faded in the presence of Father Sun. A warm breeze rippled Gundack's robe. This special day for marriages—the end of lunar waxing before the season of sandstorms—had crept beyond dawn. Gundack trudged beside Rheemar toward the crest of a rust-colored dune, his feet and legs weary from treading fine sand. Eutoebi awaited him. His tribe awaited him. Yet he stopped, panted and needed to drink again. His battle arms raised a water skin toward his parched mouth. Bitter refreshment from the last well tasted good.

"May waters of life never turn into sand," he prayed, head bowed.

"And, if they do," Rheemar said, "may heroes arise to save desert tribes from doom."

He leaned forward, arched his battle arms and climbed the next dune, his friendship arms and tail shifting. Rheemar matched his speed, taking two steps when Gundack took one. Sand dusted the human's hair and weariness filled his hazel eyes, although he hadn't complained. Rheemar would have made a good kren, despite his divided loyalties. Far better than Kan or Tarr.

Another thought of Kan. Though Tarr was fading, Gundack found that images and thoughts of Kan swirled around him.

Fortunately he felt no burning emotion. He would cultivate that absence of intensity. After all Tarr was gone, and Talla avenged. Gundack had earned the right to remarry and father an heir. Today in his homeland he would conclude the bride ceremony. Eutoebi would dwell in his tent by nightfall—if all was well and this episode in his life could end without further complications and animosity.

"How much will you pay to Eutoebi?" Rheemar said.

Rheemar had said little since their confrontation on the Mountain of the Dead. Even less since leaving the caravan behind last night at the sand-well oasis. Much had remained there, including a recuperating Sem. Carrying little more than water and silver daggers made them fleet of foot. Gundack did harbor some impatience.

"She'll set the price," Gundack said. His friendship hand fingered the baggy folds of his linen robe for the jewel pouch underneath. "Enough to care for her aging father. She is one who honors family with her love and foresight."

Gundack and she had discussed marriage over a half-year ago, before his caravan's departure to the port cities of Nath and Blane. Her price would be fair. She would not request anything for herself until their first krenling was born. That would protect Gundack's possessions from her brother's grasp. After all, who knew what debts Kan—wherever he was—owed by now? Or what unsavory krens would trek these sands to demand repayment?

Unsavory krens. According to Rheemar, one was already on the way. Yender. If only Sem and Elar were here now. But Gundack's weary sandship lizards had nearly collapsed and had needed care. Gundack took a long stride to stand atop the dune that overlooked his tribal encampment. Grit from travel coated him, as though he and the desert were one. Beyond stretched a flat expanse of rippled

"His tribe had gathered in this place of the ancestors yet again."

sand. A familiar oasis of twisted, thorny kettlefruit trees lay ahead. His tribe had gathered in this place of the ancestors yet again.

He squinted. Cloth strips, the length of a yearling pack lizard's tail, fluttered atop indigo tents in the warm morning breeze. Colorful cloth unfaded by Father Sun. Eligibility banners. No sign or smell of smoke. Yender hadn't destroyed Gundack's home. Thank Tharda. All was well and as it should be. Perhaps this day would progress according to custom.

"Thank the gods," Rheemar said, "it's all still there," as though he knew this place. "Which banner is Eutoebi's? Did she give you any clues?"

"Her banner," Gundack said, "will reflect her passion for me and our desert land."

"Anything else?" Rheemar scratched his bearded cheek. "I mean, isn't walking into a matchmaking tent the same as a preliminary marriage proposal? You better not enter the wrong one."

Gundack grunted and motioned for Rheemar to follow him down the dune. Eutoebi had provided another hint to direct him to her matchmaking tent. If he made a mistake, old krenesses would wag their spotted brown tongues and claim he wasn't clever enough to solve the courtship puzzle.

"Eyes reveal secrets," Gundack said. "That's what she told me."

"I bet her banner is the yellow one," Rheemar said, "with the red border."

"Her eyes aren't yellow," Gundack said. "They are dark as winter skies. Her banner couldn't be the yellow or pale green ones. Or the white one streaked with rust. Eutoebi would have sewn the bold banner dyed crimson and black."

"Look there," Rheemar said and pointed toward a weathered tent.

Entry flaps on the tent were shut. A marriage contract finalized. Gundack opened his eye membranes. Matchmaking had begun. And fewer banners than in previous years. What if another kren sought Eutoebi's favor?

"Isn't this too early in the day?" Rheemar asked.

"Not if a couple made prior arrangements," Gundack said.

He quickened his pace down the dune, the claw hands of his battle arms half-clenched. He should have walked the dunes faster and arrived at dawn. Yet Eutoebi had vowed to wait for him. Even her father could not force her to marry another kren until after this day had passed. She would not break her word to Gundack and dishonor her family. Dishonor him. Eutoebi wasn't like that, wasn't like Kan.

Thin curls of smoke rose from the encampment ahead. The spicy aromas of incense and talenbar wafted to Gundack's nose. He pictured the curves of Eutoebi's sensuous hips and her white belly skin, the way scales on her multi-colored scalp gleamed like jeweled vestments. Excitement rushed through him, as though his blood's desire—draped in revealing veils and plumper than ripe, sweet kettlefruit—lay before him on indigo cushions, enticing him into her four-armed embrace.

"Talenbar." Rheemar took a deep breath and laughed. He patted Gundack's arm. "The unmarried krenesses really have prepared for today. I haven't smelled that stuff burning in a fire pit for a long time. Makes me wish I was a kren."

"You almost are one," Gundack said, his eyes fixing on the silver dagger he had given Rheemar, the dagger that had been a gift from his own father.

Morning's shadows stretched across rust-colored sand. Gundack took guarded breaths as he walked, inhaling as little smoke as possible. Talenbar was an ingredient in mating potions. Tribal members would make sport if he couldn't restrain his passion in public. Gundack must control his breathing and arousal. Rheemar, on the other hand, inhaled long and slow, as though on a dare. Or yielding to an ache deep within him. Was the human dreaming about his blood's desire, yearning to stroke a young woman he had known?

"You're more than old enough," Gundack said, "to go bride shopping when you return to the Northland."

"Who would have me?" Rheemar grinned and shrugged. "I've never met a woman who begged to travel with a smelly merchant and a pack of krens."

"You're not looking in the right places," Gundack said. "Some merchant men's wives accompany their husbands everywhere."

"There was someone special." Rheemar stared into the distance. "I haven't seen her for a long while. A long while."

Gundack's tribe would rule the Red Desert until water turned to dunes. If honor prevailed, that would be a very long time. And, because of Eutoebi, Gundack's family line would continue and share in that future. Why not this young human, too?

"Perhaps," Gundack said, "you should see her again."

ⓢ   ⓢ   ⓢ

Gundack passed the refuse mound and entered the tent encampment area with Rheemar. Krens in sand-dusted, homespun robes gathered around a well. They gestured with their friendship hands as they swapped stories. Their battle arms slapped each other on the back. They drank water or kettlefruit tea from glazed pottery bowls, each volley of guffaws sending liquid dribbling down boxy chins. Nearby two male krenlings sat in the sand, casting pebble dice with their tiny six-fingered friendship hands, playing their hero games in safety. The old ways. Odors of talenbar, tea and unwashed krens mingled. Good to be home.

Rapid movement to Gundack's left drew his attention. A hooded figure darted between two tents, face turned away. Tall as a kren and wearing a long green and brown striped robe. No one in Gundack's tribe wore a hood in fair weather or robes with green stripes. Had strangers arrived? Sandship lizards roared an unfriendly greeting from beyond the tents. Their sense of smell was as sharp as their pointed teeth and spiny tails. They didn't recognize Gundack's scent. The animals must belong to krens from other tribes.

Yender might have sent his advance guards in preparation for a surprise raid. No, Yender would simply attack. Perhaps traders sought water on their journey toward a distant home or had come to seek a bride. The gods blessed all marriages sealed through tradition, even those between feuding tribes.

"Gundack," a male voice called. Robel, Talla's brother and the tribe's water-talker, approached.

"Peace and abundance," Gundack said. His battle arms embraced his brother-in-law. Then Gundack stepped backward, lifting his friendship arms to clasp the kren's outstretched hands. Robel's life pulse beat with a heavy burden.

"Travelers brought word about you finding Tarr," Robel said, reddish-brown blotches on his cheeks darker than his robe. "And, from of all places, Jular."

"The gods can bring unexpected gifts," Gundack said.

"Our north well dried up this summer." Robel's spotted tail curled and the tip twitched. "Now that you've avenged my sister Talla, surely underground streams will speak with me again and reveal a new source of water."

Gundack grunted and fingered the outline of his jewel pouch. The tribe must have been forced to purchase water, an expense most families couldn't sustain for long. No wonder so few matchmaking tents had been pitched here this year. Only kreneses who awaited the return of their chosen krens—or whose parents were too frail to migrate—would have stayed. The hooded figure could be a water merchant come to collect debts. Well, Gundack had enough star-stones to marry Eutoebi and help friends in need. But Talla's brother had opened his thoughts. Something more than water bothered him.

"Who's your friend?" Robel gestured toward Rheemar.

"Rheemar of the North," Gundack said, "a merchant. He saved Sem's life and traveled with me to the Cave of Spirit Echoes."

"May Tharda bless your stay here." Robel's friendship hands clasped Rheemar's wrists, then released them. Trepidation filled his yellow eyes. He turned his gaze back to Gundack. "It is good you plan to marry Eutoebi," Robel whispered to Gundack. "Much has happened."

Robel glanced toward the tents where the hooded figure had passed, rotating his pricked, triangular ears, until they laid flush against his head scales. He motioned for Gundack and Rheemar to come closer.

"Where are Sem and the others?" Robel asked.

"We left everyone at the sand-well oasis," Rheemar said. He took a quick look over his shoulder. "Zel and the other lizards were exhausted."

"There's more," Robel said. "Three strangers from a mountain tribe arrived yesterday. They brought two drivers and two slaves."

Was Yender one of the strangers? Was one of the drivers or slaves Rheemar's captured blood ally? Could Jardeen be among them?

"What tribal ring do they wear?" Gundack said.

"Not bloodstone bands," Robel said. "At least, not the two I could see. Their rings were silver, so they're probably from the Chalk Mountains. One odd thing. Their slaves wore molders hoods. And long green and brown striped robes."

So the hooded kren was a slave from the Chalk Mountains. Gundack had been there several moon cycles ago. An arduous landscape. Even more demanding for molders survivors to travel, their ravaged bodies buried under heavy cloth, seeing the world through only two small holes.

"Was one of the slaves a human?" Rheemar said and swallowed hard. "Perhaps a woman?"

"I think so," Robel said. "The scent suggested as much. They kept that one at a distance."

"Did you notice anything?" Rheemar said. "See anything odd at all about her?"

"The right hand was gone," Robel said.

"Oh, dear Tharda." The human lowered his head and cradled his bearded face against his hand. "Jardeen."

"His sister." Gundack's gaze met Robel's. "Her safety is of much concern to us both."

Molders ate away human or clawkren flesh. Faces, scales, breasts—the disease spared nothing, given the opportunity. If Jardeen truly had molders, what else would have been eaten away? Gundack stretched his friendship arm across Rheemar's shoulders.

"What about Eutoebi?" Gundack said. "Have any strangers troubled her?"

"Last night," Robel said, "I heard a cry from her tent. She and the strangers exchanged strong words. I entered to protect her. Three mountain krens apologized and left. I think those vermin plot to buy Zydra."

Zydra? The kreness of chalk? Had Eutoebi's good friend reached marriageable age already? A white cloth banner, pale as Zydra's skin and scales, rippled above a nearby tent. Talla's brother must be right.

Gundack rubbed the back of his neck. Krens took chalk-krenesses within their own tribe for helper wives. Strangers purchased unpigmented krenesses for only one reason—their slight build and delicate features brought a good price in port-city pleasure dens. These mountain krens of the silver rings must not be permitted to dishonor Zydra and her father.

"Gather what elders you can," Gundack said to Robel. Tension faded from Robel's yellow eyes. "The old ones must select a husband for Zydra. I want the choosing made before high sun."

"I've got to find Jardeen," Rheemar said. His warm hand touched the back of Gundack's waist.

"There's a stirred pot of trouble brewing," Gundack said. "Watch your back and keep your daggers handy."

"I intend to," Rheemar said.

"May Tharda's white light bring you strength," Gundack whispered.

Gundack inhaled a whiff of incense, almost feeling the caress of Eutoebi's spotted tongue. Time to enter Eutoebi's tent and get her safely married, in case deceitful mountain vermin went bride-shopping in her direction. Later, he would deal with the krens of the silver rings and ensure Zydra's safety. For now, his own desire was enough.

CHAPTER TWENTY-FOUR

A DIFFERENT PRICE

Gundack bent, entered Eutoebi's tent, and straightened, his friendship hands together. Before him, halfway across the floor, Eutoebi knelt on an indigo cushion near her elderly father, her spotted lips closed in a thin smile. The graceful curve of her face framed two captivating eyes and high-set cheekbones. The tips of her triangular green ears pointed in his direction. Her crimson head scales gleamed like polished gems. Gundack inhaled as though to absorb Eutoebi's beauty within his being.

"Thank the gods," Eutoebi whispered, clasping her petite friendship hands against her scarlet robe. "Oh, Gundack."

Blood pounded within his temples and neck. The aroma of smoldering talenbar seeped into every corner of his mind. He wanted to close the tent flap. But, on this day of marriages, only Eutoebi or her father had that right. They would shut out other suitors after the proper number of starstones had changed hands. Now Gundack must perform all parts of the expected ritual.

"It is time," Gundack said, "to combine our two futures in a single teapot."

He fumbled for the pouch under his robe. Eutoebi nodded and crumbled dried cragweed. Her friendship fingers blended his leaves with her own. Such a lingering fragrance. A good omen.

Her father huddled in a blanket on a woven brown carpet. His head scales and deep amber eyes lacked luster. Father Sun no longer blessed the old kren with the gift of divine energy. In advanced age, this condition never improved. This kren's spirit would join Talla's before the next season of blossoms. Concern replaced Gundack's mating arousal.

"Your father—" Gundack said.

"You settled matters with Talla?" Eutoebi asked. She wrapped a square of hide around the handle of an iron water kettle and removed the vessel from the heating stone.

"She approves of you," Gundack said. "I think many spirits approve of our union."

"Oh," she said, lowering her voice.

Eutoebi poured tea into three glazed pottery bowls. One of her family arms nudged a tray of nuts and dried kettlefruit wedges across the rug in his direction. Last year, her four hands had woven this carpet. How agile those clawless hands were compared to his own. She took slow yet shallow breaths, as though resisting the seductive power of talenbar. If only he could read her life pulse. No, that would come later in the ceremony, when they shared their vows of loyalty and honor. Now she awaited his formal proposal, the traditional words.

Gundack knelt on a woven mat next to Eutoebi's father and faced his blood's desire. His friendship hands raised one bowl of tea to the old kren's mouth, according to courtship customs. The gray head tilted back and drank. Gundack might be equally frail when his and Eutoebi's krenlings reached marrying age. He glanced at Eutoebi—barely two years past krenlinghood. Did she really find him attractive or did she seek security? No matter. He would secure her safety as well as that of their progeny. He offered Eutoebi a bowl of tea to complete the first part of the ritual. Then Gundack lifted the third bowl toward his own mouth, bending his neck down to reach the sweet liquid. His friendship arms were a little shorter than those of most krens. Usually, the difference didn't cross his mind. This time he felt again the awkwardness, but finished the tea.

He set the empty bowl on the carpet. She pushed the tray of nuts and kettlefruit still closer. An encouragement or formality? Should he eat something now or wait until after he proposed? With Talla, he had eaten first. Yet such behavior, expected of a younger kren, might not please Eutoebi. The talenbar eroded his confidence. An odd sensation tingled the back of Gundack's neck. He had braved sandstorms, faced the deadly claws of raider krens in close combat, entered the Cave of Spirit Echoes. How could the nearness of this kreness now engulf him in such daunting dunes of uncertainty? Gundack placed a kettlefruit wedge, studded with his favorite insects, in his cupped hand. Now for the words of his father and grandfathers, words to give his life new purpose and meaning.

"You are my blood's desire," Gundack said, fingering the kettlefruit. Each syllable rang within his mind, like delicate bells on bridles of sandship lizards. "What is your marriage price?"

Eutoebi's glance met his, turned away and then returned. The tip of her first finger rimmed the pottery tea bowl. She hesitated. Why? Nothing within tradition prescribed such delay. Her pleasant, spicy scent offered no clue.

"Five sandship lizards," she said, her voice small as a grain of sand, her eyes tracking his. Then her eyelids lowered, as though a heavy weight tugged them.

Five sandship lizards. Five. The kettlefruit section dropped from Gundack's grasp. Five loyal, experienced pack animals. Had Eutoebi really said that? Brides asked for a handful of starstones or silver coins. Eutoebi was worth all of that and more. But half of Gundack's entire herd? Even one sandship lizard—young and totally untrained—would cost far more than any bride's rightful request.

"You ask for five sandships," Gundack said. "Your dying father isn't going to take up trading this late in life. How can you ask this? I might as well give them directly to Kan."

Had she intentionally set a price he would refuse? Had she become the blood's desire of another kren? Gundack folded both sets of arms against his body. Something had happened since he and Eutoebi had last discussed marriage. But, wait. She had requested a price he could afford. If Eutoebi had sought a prompt refusal, she would have asked for eleven sandship lizards—more than he owned. He straightened his tail, shifted backward and sat on his heels.

"Five," she said, her voice low and firm, pleading eyes more piercing than sharpened claws.

"You need to explain," Gundack said, still kneeling, his voice louder than before.

Eutoebi pressed one finger against her spotted lips and gestured toward her father. The old kren, eyes closed, curled on his side. What was she trying to conceal from him?

"I can say no more here," she whispered. Her dark eyes had no sparkle, as though burdened by great sorrow. "Zydra knows all. You are the only kren I could ever want to marry. Please believe me."

At least she still favored him. But Eutoebi must need money. Her father could owe heavy debts to water merchants. Raiders might have captured her brother, Kan, and maybe those krens from another tribe had brought a ransom demand. He must ensure that marriage negotiations with Eutoebi remained open. Zydra knew all. Gundack needed to talk with Zydra. Now.

Gundack withdrew his jewel pouch and fumbled with the drawstrings. He placed a sparkling blue starstone, the size of a small round nut, inside his tea bowl. This would show he planned to bargain for a different price, that he still intended to marry Eutoebi today.

"I'll speak with Zydra and return." Gundack stood and secured the jewel pouch back under his robe. "I'll work out a plan. And I won't enter her tent. You are my only blood's desire."

ᔅ ᔅ ᔅ

Long quick strides took Gundack along the sandy path toward the encampment's center. He called to Robel. The thick-waisted kren turned, squinted and pricked his ears, a display of surprise.

"Some sort of trouble's festering," Gundack said. "I must know the circumstances before a price can be set."

This kren always supported Gundack. Loyalty and trust were essential now, as they had been in his search for Tarr and pilgrimage to the mountain. If Tarr's family or Kan had spawned new treachery, the trouble would end here.

"Permit no other krens to approach Eutoebi," Gundack said. "Particularly the strangers."

"What about the elders?" Robel said. "The choosing? I have arranged it all for Zydra."

"That must wait," Gundack said. "I go to Zydra now for another purpose."

"Then I'll guard Eutoebi well," Robel said. "I vow."

Gundack strode past a kettlefruit tree with thick, drooping leaves. Ahead, a bride's white banner fluttered in the breeze. He stuck his head into the opening of the tent. Zydra's elderly father lay on a crumpled robe. She knelt on a flat brown cushion, facing sideways, both sets of pale hands weaving a sleeping mat on a small loom. Her unveiled white skin appeared softer, thinner than he had recalled. Pale chestnut tinged the areas around her eyelids and mouth, where blood ran just beneath the surface. Her eyes were cast toward the ceiling.

Something was wrong here, too. Rich carpets and indigo cushions no longer decorated her tent. No cobalt blue water jars. No stack of folded linen robes. Even her tall carpet loom—the source of income for her family—was missing. And no tray of food, no silver tea vessel and set of pottery bowls, lay waiting to greet a suitor—or any guest at all.

"Water merchants," Zydra said, as though reading his mind.

He motioned for Zydra to come to the entry flap. She rose and walked toward him, ears flattened, her expression as pained as Eutoebi's had been.

"Eutoebi sent me to talk to you."

"I'm so sorry," Zydra said, looking up at him, little more than half his height. Her friendship hands, as delicate as those on a carved doll, clasped his. "The spirits. May they aid Eutoebi. Somehow."

"What do you mean?" Gundack stiffened. "What danger seeks Eutoebi?"

"Oh, dear Tharda," she whispered, her pink eyes almost wide enough to peer into his soul. "She didn't tell you? You don't know?"

Zydra stepped away from him and raised her family hands. She rested her thumbs against her jaws and spread each set of three thin fingers across her eyes, pale cheeks and nose. She hid behind her hands. She couldn't look at him.

"Of what do you speak?" Gundack said, the grasp of fear tightening within him.

"The krens of the silver rings." Zydra sank to her knees, her voice rising into a pitiful long wail. "Kan sold her. In the mountains. A moon cycle ago."

"Kan. Kan sold Eutoebi? How?"

A hot flush shot though Gundack, as though sharpened claws of an unseen assailant slashed into his muscles. True, an unmarried kreness was the property of her father and brothers. They even had some claim to her possessions until her first heir was born. Those conditions were and always had been part of the laws of desert and mountain krens. Yet the gods had meant for krenesses to choose their own husbands. Only a monster would sell his own sister or daughter against her will or for his own gain. What had Kan become?

Gundack stepped back from the entrance to Zydra's tent and strode toward Eutoebi's, his bare feet pounding warm sand. He had to stop those wretched krens. His blood's desire mustn't concede to their demands. He mustn't let those vermin stroke her belly—force themselves against her. He had to reason with them, threaten them. Whatever worked. Robel would back him up. But the tent appeared before him with the flap lowered. Closed. A marriage contract had been finalized. Witnessed and blessed by the gods. How could this be? Eutoebi was his. Talla had given her approval.

"Gundack," Robel said, "I was powerless to stop them."

Talla's brother just stood there, in front of him, battle arms at his sides. Why had Robel broken his promise and permitted another kren to pass? How could this have happened? A fire seized him. Gundack lunged for the entry flap. Robel's strong arms grabbed Gundack and yanked him sideways. Gundack's feet skidded. His tail and right battle arm thrashed in one direction, then another as he fought to regain balance. Gundack tumbled to the ground, bringing his brother-in-law with him.

"Eutoebi is to wed a mountain chieftain," Robel shouted, still clutching him. "Where is your honor? Do you want war?"

Images of burning tents flashed through Gundack's mind. Krenlings wailing in anguish over parents' crumpled bodies. Warriors dragging terrified orphans away. Robel was right. Gundack had witnessed such horrors as had Robel. No desert or mountain tribe started war over accepted matters of vengeance. That was why he had pursued Tarr within the constraints of customs. But matters of marriage were sacred. Matters of marriage could and did start wars. Kan—wherever he was, whatever he had done—had sealed a contract and accepted a price. This marriage was inviolable. The matter was settled.

Gundack drew himself into a sitting position, his head lowered. Eutoebi had not wanted five sandship lizards for a bride price. She had only needed him to leave her tent. She had accepted her fate, then shared her last moments of freedom with him, leaving her tent flap open to allow them time together. Then she had kept him from jeopardy by sending him off to Zydra. Eutoebi had said goodbye to Gundack in her own way and sacrificed her own happiness to spare their tribe from war.

"I saw the contract," Robel said. "When you were with Zydra. Sealed with the silver amulet Kan stole from you, from our tribe. I knew Eutoebi interested the mountain krens, but, until then, never suspected Kan had traveled to the mountains and sold her." He knelt beside Gundack, clenched fist pressed against bowed forehead. "Please forgive me."

Gundack nodded. How had this happened? Why had Kan done this to Eutoebi? To him. Shadows on the dunes. Somehow, Yender was involved. Then an angry male voice shouted. A kreness yelled.

Gundack turned. The sounds had not arisen from Eutoebi's tent. Might the other mountain vermin now threaten Zydra?

Gundack leaped to his feet, his four arms flailing for balance, and hurried toward Zydra's tent. The flaps were still open. He lunged through the entrance, dug his claws into the back of a mountain kren's robe, then into the scoundrel's flesh.

"Gundack, no." Zydra knelt on a cushion and stared at him with wild pink eyes.

"Don't you understand?" Gundack shouted, all the peace he had found with the web-threaders gone. "This is slavery. Eutoebi would never want this for you."

A howl erupted from Gundack. He must prevail. He spun the mountain kren around, dragged him outside and thrust him onto the red sand. Chestnut blood flowed from the kren's shoulder. An emerald bloodstone band, a ring, glistened on one of the kren's claw fingers. This kren didn't live in the Chalk Mountains. He was a member of Tarr's tribe.

CHAPTER TWENTY-FIVE

HEROES ARISE

The injured mountain kren cowered in the sand, his expression tight with pain. Yet he made no sound or utterance. Gundack's pulse raced. What was the meaning of all this? Could the euphoria he'd experienced in the Cave of Spirit Echoes be so ephemeral that the first signs of tribal rivalries would dissolve it? And the beauty the web-threader had shown him, that too could fade like embers doused with water. The heat of anger and revenge filled him again, as completely as the murder of Talla had ten years before.

"Zydra is mine," Gundack shouted. "Go back to the others. To your own filthy tribe. Each season of blossoms I'll scour the port cities. All cities. I'll seek out every den of pleasure. I'll check every kreness's face. If you or your friends dishonor Eutoebi, I'll bring her home. Then I'll hunt all of you and slash your bodies to shreds. If it takes me the rest of my life, this will happen."

The kren, notch ears flattened, writhed on the ground. His amber eyes seethed with hatred and fear. He pressed the palm of one claw hand against his gaping wound. The yellow tinge to his claws was like Tarr's. The odd yellowing of his head scales was, too. And youthfulness accented his boxy face. This had to be Yender. Oh, dear Tharda. Tarr's brother and two dishonorable allies, not a chieftain from the Chalk Mountains, now owned Eutoebi. Yender or his family had planned revenge against Gundack, retribution within the scope of tribal laws. Societal wounds inflicted by this twisted scheme would fester for generations. A price Gundack had never anticipated.

A soft rustle drew his attention to the indigo tent behind Yender. A hooded figure in a green and brown striped robe emerged from behind hide flaps. Too tall for the human woman Jardeen, this must be the slave Gundack had noticed earlier, the one Robel had seen with Rheemar's sister. Penetrating eyes, dark as Eutoebi's, stared in his direction. Eyes revealing secrets. Yet most certainly coming to the aid of the master.

The hooded kren displayed clawless finger-stubs on his battle hands. Mutilation due to slavery. Yet one of his friendship hands clasped an object, half-hidden in the folds of his robe. A metal blade. A knife. The type used by krenesses to slice kettlefruit or melons. The slave kren raised one friendship hand, fingers spread. A plea for Gundack to do no further harm to Tarr's brother? Or to attempt a strike? This one was no more than a krenling in a full-grown body. Less able than a human against a kren. Gundack, remembering the harm he'd done to Tarr's krenling, halted.

Yender, still bleeding on the ground, faced Gundack and raised himself to his knees. Had he not heard his slave's movement behind him? The slave would aid his master. And a crowd gathered. Somewhere soon in that crowd Yender's companions would appear. The krens of the silver rings would take immediate action when they saw Yender. But Yender attempted to rise to his feet on his own. Fury must have clouded Yender's instincts.

Gundack arched his battle arms, ready for whatever might happen. Certainly Yender's fellow krens were a real threat. Then the slave kren made the first move, lifting his knife and lunging forward. Gundack anticipated the weak attack and stepped to the side. But the slave didn't come at him. Instead he used the force of both of his friendship arms to drive the blade through Yender's thick neck.

A cry erupted from Tarr's brother. Fresh blood spurted from his wound. Yender's hand went to his throat as if to staunch the flow. An expression of horror filled his face. Then the kren toppled forward and collapsed face down, his life fluid pulsing onto the red sand. Smells of blood and released gases filled the air. Sound seemed to vanish. Gundack stood frozen. This was murder.

The slave stumbled backward, then sank to his knees, the stubs of his clawless battle hands clasped. The slave had committed murder in full view of all. The still-hooded slave would be an easy target for Tarr's allies from the Chalk Mountains. This was no longer Gundack's problem. Let others take their vengeance in this matter in the prescribed way. Gundack's heart carried enough grief.

"I never wanted things to end this way," the slave said, his voice edged with fear. "This was never my intention."

The slave tore off his molders hood. His disease-scarred face lacked a cheek and half a nose, as though a crazed sandship lizard had once tried to eat him alive. Only his dark eyes remained unharmed. The slave pressed his hood against his master's wound, slipping one hand between the kren's throat and the ground. Blackened skin hung flaccid on his battle arms. The worst case of molders Gundack had ever seen. New grief filled him.

A kreness screamed. Eutoebi. She had heard the commotion. Gundack turned. She stood within a cluster of krens, gathered beyond Zydra's tent. Two strangers in red and black striped robes appeared at the same edge of the gathering and pushed aside the crowd, heading in the slave and Gundack's direction. These must be the krens of the silver rings, the traitors who now owned Eutoebi. Eutoebi struggled to move with them. What was she doing?

"Stop," Eutoebi shouted. One of the strangers glanced back over his shoulder. "You promised Kan could live and take care of my father. You let me add that to the contract. Made it part of my price."

Eutoebi darted after them. Why was she shouting about Kan? A group of older krenesses grabbed and restrained her. She twisted her arms, her entire body. The krenesses held her fast. Still she struggled.

"If Kan dies," Eutoebi yelled, "my vow of marriage is broken." She raised all of her arms as if to grasp air. "Let my brother live."

Her brother. Kan. This disfigured slave was Kan. Whispers and rasps spread through the gathered crowd. His eyes, yes, were as dark as Eutoebi's. And one of the mountain krens had shown Robel the silver amulet Kan had stolen. But such a molders-eaten face. How could she—anyone—be certain?

The two mountain krens moved toward the slave, sharp claws ready to strike. They would rip the flesh from Kan's bones. Tear out his eyes. A shiver shot through Gundack. They would leave Kan shredded, as Tarr had done to Talla. And vengeance would beget more vengeance. If these two slew Kan, this tribe would slash the stranger's throats. Kan had killed Tarr's brother probably with good reason. Desert kren justice would stand on his side. No matter. These mountain krens in turn would have the right to kill him. And more retaliation would follow.

Winds would carry the fateful message of this wretched matter. More would find justification to exact revenge. What next? War. Kan's death would return Eutoebi to Gundack, but what horrific future would their krenlings face? Yet, if these mountain krens let Kan live, they would return to their own tribe in shame. They would spread the story of Kan's deed to Tarr's tribe. Yender's family would poison desert wells and restrict the travel of water merchants. Or they would plot with those merchants to destroy the desert clawkren. Only some form of retribution would restore their honor. Honor would beget vengeance which would beget more vengeance.

Gundack had the right to kill Kan and settle this matter now. That didn't make that act right or honorable. And would it save Eutoebi? She might never forgive him for killing Kan, nor see the panorama of deaths he could envision. He turned his eyes to the lifeless mountain kren. Chestnut blood from the lifeless Yender darkened the ground. The liquid seeped through rust-colored sand as though waters of life turned into dunes. This was the ancient curse. At the heart of the water prayer. Water into dunes. Gundack must do something to prevent disaster.

"Stand back," a kreness commanded.

The voice was firm, familiar, but not Eutoebi's. Zydra, the kreness of chalk, strode through shallow sand. She pulled her petite body to full height, head raised high. No veils covered her head, neck and arms, as though she defied Father Sun to burn her scales and flesh.

"This is not your fight," one of the mountain krens shouted. "Go back to your tent."

"It is her fight," a human said. Rheemar. "It's my fight, too."

Rheemar emerged from the tent behind Kan and stared at the prostrate body of Yender. Anguish washed across his face. He hunched forward, arms spread and legs apart, gripping two silver daggers. His hazel eyes glared and his slight frame towered over the crouching Kan. He had once told Gundack he would fight for the desert. His voice held that determination now.

"Anyone who kills Kan," Rheemar shouted, "dies." A rising breeze fluttered his yellow robe. Sweat beaded on his forehead. "Kan is my blood brother."

Kan, Rheemar's blood brother. Gundack's breath caught in his throat. How could Kan—this miserable slave—be Rheemar's blood ally? But it must be true. Rheemar had said so. And he was ready to fight the two krens of the silver rings, a battle he couldn't possibly survive without assistance. Rheemar had the honor of a desert kren.

"Let Zydra pass," Gundack ordered, motioning with all four arms. He must defend the kreness of chalk as well as Rheemar, whose arteries pulsed with the blood of Eutoebi's family. Gundack spread his battle arms wide, palms turned skyward. "Oh, mighty sands and waters, be her strength. And if you won't, I will."

The kreness of chalk moved with forceful steps, mouth pinched shut. One of the notch-eared krens who had purchased Eutoebi grabbed her pale arm. She pushed the kren, twice her size, away. His flattened ears and wide amber eyes projected terror. Did he now understand and share Gundack's fears for the future? Or had he envisioned something worse?

"Return to your own tent," Zydra said to him.

The mountain kren removed the silver ring from his claw hand and replaced it with another band. He raised his battle arm. Sunlight shone on polished emerald bloodstone. He wasn't from the Chalk Mountains either. He was a member of Tarr's tribe. Gundack stepped forward, prepared to block the way between the notch-eared kren and Rheemar.

"Rheemar," the mountain kren shouted. "When I avenge Yender, will you kill even me?"

"If you avenge Yender," Rheemar called to the mountain kren, "you had better prepare to die with me."

"No," a feminine voice said.

Another human—a woman—with flowing ebony hair and an angular, unscarred face moved behind Rheemar. Her blue-gray eyes opened wide. A withered, blackened stump protruded from her arm, where one hand should have been. Jardeen. She didn't have molders, but by the looks of that stump, she'd had sucker slimes. Tarr must have infested her fingernails with slimes, and let them rot her hand until she begged for the amputation.

"Stay back, Jardeen," Rheemar commanded, motioning with one of his daggers. "Don't you understand? This day I must be a desert kren."

"Do as your brother asks," Gundack called to Jardeen. "If you want to help, pray. Pray for an ancient hero to arise. Pray that no irreparable damage will be done here. That vengeance will not swallow the land."

Zydra pushed past in front of Gundack and stopped at Yender's lifeless body. Her family and friendship hands tugged together to dislodge the knife. Chestnut blood oozed from the wound and coated her hands. Blood stained her homespun lavender robe. She lifted the weapon above her head and turned toward Kan.

"Hero arise," she whispered.

Kan tilted his disfigured face upward, his dark eyes brimming with emotion. He rose to his feet and pressed something into her hand. Crimson cording. Kan extended his own friendship arms, as though asking her to read him. Zydra placed the knife in his open

" 'Hero arise,' she whispered."

palm, blade pointed toward his stomach. She closed his friendship fingers around the hilt.

"Save us," she said, "from ourselves. Free Eutoebi from a life of misery. Give us peace so your sister's krenlings—all of our krenlings—may be born in these ancestral sands in peace."

Zydra stepped backward, her profile as formidable as the Mountain of the Dead. She slipped the circle of crimson cording around her head. Silver glinted from a small bloodstained oval against her robe. Gundack's water amulet. The charm's power radiated to where he stood. Zydra lifted her chin, as though she claimed the amulet for her own.

This was not the meek kreness of chalk Gundack had known. This was the white kreness of Tharda's light. Tarr and his wife had believed their chalk krenling was the white light, the gift from Tharda. But Zydra was the one who could bring strength to the least of them and save the clawkren.

Kan turned his head. His eyes searched Gundack's. Eutoebi screamed. A sick feeling washed through Gundack. Kan must do this. And Eutoebi must not see this. She must not witness Kan's death.

"Let my brother live," Eutoebi said. She rushed forward and grasped Gundack's battle arm.

"Let him choose honor," Gundack said. "Let him climb above his weakest point and clean the stains on his honor. I have walked the Cave of Spirit Echoes. Honor is the seed of hope. The well-water of our future."

"Then I must be near him," Eutoebi whispered. "That must be part of my bride price."

"Stand with me, then," Gundack said. He stretched one battle arm around her and pressed the side of her face against his chest.

Zydra stood in front of Kan, her legs apart and head held high, family arms stretched straight out sideways, friendship arms pointed forward, all four palms raised. A command for none to pass her or stop Kan. Sunlight gleamed around her. She could have made the very sands speak.

More than the sands needed to speak. Kan knew what he had to do but struggled to find courage. Gundack's time to find courage had come. He who did not believe in heroes must call one forth as a soothsayer had once predicted.

"Kan," Gundack said. "Much has happened between us. Years ago, I trusted you. You betrayed me. Now you have returned my water amulet to our tribe. And you hold our futures in your hands. You have made choices. Make the next one, too." Gundack listened to a memory of the drone of web-threaders in that distant mountain cavern. Yes, they would give him strength. "When Eutoebi and I tell our krenlings about you, we will speak of a brave kren who prevented war. Those other things, they are of no consequence anymore. Just insignificant grains of sand blown away by wind. You have earned both forgiveness and peace, my brother."

"Am I not to see the ending days of my father or the beginning days of my sister's krenlings?" Kan's voice was weak.

"You will," Gundack answered. "But not in this body that holds you now."

"Yes," Rheemar said. "Walk with Tharda. You will be my brother in eternity. May you join the spirits' breath."

Kan turned his marred face down toward Yender's body. His friendship hands clasped the knife tighter. His mutilated battle hands curved around unblemished fingers. All of him prepared to die. And, with the same deliberation and power with which he had plunged a knife into Yender's neck, he moved the point, then the length of the shaft into the softness of his own belly.

Kan's low-pitched groan tightened Gundack's stomach muscles. A soft thud and the smell of fresh blood followed. Kan folded over Yender's body. The murmur of a prayer rumbled in low bass tones among those gathered. Rheemar stepped forward and opened his palms to the morning sky as though offering to be read by Tharda herself. Then he knelt beside the two dead krens and wept.

Eutoebi slipped her friendship hands into Gundack's. Her life pulse throbbed with a rapid rhythm. Rasps and wails of mourning poured from her and filled the air—sand scratching a moaning wind of sorrow. May the pain he felt within her now eventually bleed from her soul the way her brother's blood now drained into the Red Sands. Then she would know as he did that Kan had been a hero, called forth as they all had been this day.